JAMES I. MCGOVERN

A novel
___
Beyond the Failure Club

Outskirts Press, Inc.
Denver, Colorado

This is a work of fiction. The events and characters described here are imaginary and are not intended to refer to specific places or living persons. The opinions expressed in this manuscript are solely the opinions of the author and do not represent the opinions or thoughts of the publisher. The author represents and warrants that s/he either owns or has the legal right to publish all material in this book.

Beyond the Failure Club
A Novel
All Rights Reserved
Copyright © 2007 James I. McGovern

Cover Image © 2007 JupiterImages Corporation
All Rights Reserved. Used With Permission.

This book may not be reproduced, transmitted, or stored in whole or in part by any means, including graphic, electronic, or mechanical without the express written consent of the publisher except in the case of brief quotations embodied in critical articles and reviews.

Outskirts Press
http://www.outskirtspress.com

ISBN-10: 1-4327-0120-7
ISBN-13: 978-1-4327-0120-8

Library of Congress Control Number: 2006938461

Outskirts Press and the "OP" logo are trademarks belonging to Outskirts Press, Inc.

Printed in the United States of America

CHAPTER 1

He seemed too isolated, too self-satisfied, to ever become a terrorist, but maybe that's what qualified him.

His name was Byron Invictus, but he was usually called Bar by his few acquaintances. He was formerly Chester Tracz, denizen of a crumbling ethnic neighborhood in Chicago. He'd lived briefly in Colorado, but he'd returned and was settled now in northern Indiana. He worked as the evening case manager at Five-County Rehab and Counseling, just outside Flag City. He was having a non-sexual relationship with a woman named Ulitreé, who was a sales clerk at Primal Dream, which specialized in health products and New Age solutions.

Bar's work at Five-County was largely clerical, since most therapy sessions and visits to in-patients were during the daytime. There were occasional calls from the police, but these were minimal since Five-County was not a secure facility. Bar thus had a lot of free time. He spent most of it at his computer, surfing wide and deep to find non-religious meaning in life.

It was on an evening during summer, the fading orange sky casting shadows through the office, that Bar made his first contact. He'd riffled through articles on modern futility, confining cultural values, and the like, most of them too academic to be useful. He read about self-help, support and discussion groups, and browsed into the unconventional, the radical. He was about to click away from a secular humanist website when one of their links caught his eye: "The Failure Club." He wondered at this. Why a club? Looking away through the empty office into the pre-dusk, he was amused by a premonition: It was actually out there, a group in which he could relate. He clicked the link.

They met once a month at the Galactic Retreat Center near the town of Argentina, with an alternate venue at the Argentina Public Library, conference room. They didn't meet just to talk, stressed the website, but to decide on actions to take. These could include supporting unpopular causes and fringe candidates. Benefits of membership included group discounts on various material pleasures. To join, one registered to attend the next meeting by emailing a form to Dr. Lyme, secretary. "See you there!"

The drive would be around 150 miles, Bar reflected, mostly south toward Indy but east a ways, too. An overnighter. But a retreat center, so there'd be facilities. Not if it's at the library, though. Maybe I should kick it around with Ulitreé, see if she wants to make the trip. If not, what the hell, that'll just make it easier. Nothing about fees, I see.

Ulitreé was in her thirties, somewhat younger than Bar, and had once been a nudist. She'd believed in the non-sexual beauty of the body, but as she grew older she was nagged by doubts. She was tall with dark blond hair and, to Bar, she was still attractive. But she allowed him no more than friendship because, while the nudism was gone, the non-sexuality remained. Bar hoped for further evolution. He had few social contacts so, for now, Ulitreé was his "significant other," required by the culture to avoid weirdo status.

"Doesn't seem to be much to it," she said of the Failure Club. "Especially considering the drive."

"Well, I could only tell so much from the website. You really have to *be* there to judge, I think. I thought it might be something for us to share—just checking it out, I mean. The time on the road together."

She looked at him as if waiting for more.

"I can see the road angle, but the destination doesn't do it for me, Bar. Why don't you check it out and we'll say maybe next time for me?"

He hadn't even gotten to the separate sleeping issue. Bar could feel hurt, if he chose, but he preferred traveling alone, anyway. So he let it drop with Ulitreé and registered for one via email to Dr. Lyme, secretary.

It was a pleasant evening when he took off for the meeting, cooler than normal though still rather humid. The low sun was casting its soft orange glow as he turned off the highway. It was another twenty miles to Argentina, with the Galactic Retreat Center preceding the town. Reached by a long gravel driveway, it consisted of a single barn-like building with a small addition on one end. It had faded white paint and greenish shingles. There was a motley assortment of vehicles parked in an adjacent field, including some campers. So much for accommodations, Bar thought.

He parked on the outskirts of the field and got out warily, as was his habit. While he hadn't yet seen anyone, he now noticed some movement and noises at the edge of the nearby woods. As he watched from behind his car, a stocky woman sprinted out with a squealing laugh, her blouse half off. A stocky man lumbered after her, sporting a lascivious grin. He was soon clutching her from behind, fondling and kissing.

"There's the meeting," she protested.

"Yeah, the meeting."

She began to return his affection but he suddenly raised his head. He looked to the building with a sober expression, released his lover, and gave her a butt-slap.

"Let's go."

They walked off past the vehicles, the woman adjusting her blouse. Bar followed at a discreet distance.

The interior of the building was mostly one big space, with folding chairs and about two dozen people waiting for something to happen. A table with coffee pots, soda, and cookies was set up in the rear. In the front, some sort of banner was hung behind several chairs that faced the main group. The banner featured an orange symbol on a purple background, the symbol consisting of a *V* resting on a line inside a circle.

"Mr. Invictus, I presume?"

A man in a plaid sports coat pinned Bar with his smile. He had styled sandy hair and goatee, with tan plastic frames on his glasses.

"I'm Dr. Lyme. Welcome to the Failure Club."

Bar smiled at the words and Lyme took it as camaraderie, giving Bar's hand an outrageous pumping.

"Don't worry, I'm a chiropractor. I can adjust anything I knock out of place."

"No problem. How did you know me?"

"You're the only new face. Thanks for following our registration procedure."

"Oh, I always follow procedure," Bar smiled.

This time Lyme caught Bar's meaning and smiled also. He also glimpsed the amulet Bar was wearing: a pentacle engraved on crystal, a gift from Ulitreé.

"Come," said Lyme, "let's meet some of the others."

Bar was introduced to the treasurer, Mr. Singh, who was standing nearby, and to some members who were conversing in twos and threes. There was Marlena, a middle-aged realtor who had trouble keeping her license. She was talking with Mr. Tongor, whose restaurant partner had liquidated their business and disappeared. Moving into the hall, Dr. Lyme pointed out Collins, a tall man chuckling at the stories of a rotund trucker named Bo.

"Collins was a hippie once, but always rather private,

individual. Joined the Air Force while high on marijuana. Discharged as a schizoid. Worked on the docks till his back gave out. Very bright guy, just erratic. Like a lot of us. But, maybe by getting together we can get our individual selves together."

Bar grunted. He wasn't here for therapy, if that's what this was about. He worked in the field already. But he sensed something else here, less structured and prying. If he could expand himself, connect with a few people, maybe he'd have more to offer Ulitreé, from the club as well as himself. Maybe then they could be intimate.

"Holding court over here," said Lyme, "is Mr. Bechfield, script writer for soap operas. His disciples are Gene Reed and Vyetta."

Bechfield was wearing a robe and slippers for some reason. Gene Reed was an anxious young man, Vyetta heavy-set and saturnine.

"There are really just four or five stories," said Bechfield. "You can only chew them up and spit them out so many different ways."

"I have some digestive enzymes I can recommend," Lyme told him. Then to Bar, "I'm also a naprapath."

From a safe distance Lyme mentioned Lar Cody, who had run a federal facility until arrested as a pedophile. Half-turned to him was Okkura, a masseuse having trouble with prostitution arrests. Closer to Lyme and Bar was an alcoholic couple, Janus and Kitty, who was either older or more advanced than her male companion. They were listening to Charybdis, a very heavy woman who was suing her employer over reasonable accommodation, something involving time off and a heavy-duty chair not up to specs.

"There are all kinds of failures here," said Lyme, "and some who are only failures in their own minds, or who want to prevent failure or just study it, to know it. Here's The Private coming in. Real name's Tom, but everyone goes by the handle they want here."

Bar found himself facing the man he'd seen outside, chasing and fondling the stocky woman. Dr. Lyme introduced them.

"I'll have to run the meeting, Bar. I'll hand you off to The Private for now. He's been with us quite a while. A veteran twice over."

"Xyntius ain't coming?"

"Something came up again. Academic hassles."

"Shit. Man has to understand priorities. What's so important?"

"It was Hilda who called. His secretary. She didn't say exactly."

The Private stared into space.

"Hilda," he mused.

Lyme broke away and headed toward the facing chairs at the front. An elderly man had already sat in one of the chairs facing the members. Mr. Singh joined them and Dr. Lyme called the meeting to order. Bar took a seat next to The Private.

"Old guy's our vice-president, Judge Waters," The Private explained. "He ain't really a judge now. Resigned, retired. Whatever."

"The one who's not coming—the president?"

"Yeah, Xyntius. He's a doctor too, but the bullshit professor kind. Can't even get here 'cause of that crap they muck around in."

Dr. Lyme was rehashing an unresolved issue from the last meeting. As far as Bar could tell, it involved a possible campaign for single-class air travel, eliminating first class, business class, and any others.

"This is all bullshit," The Private informed him.

The members had little to add to the rehashing, so Lyme tabled the matter for Dr. Xyntius's return.

"We'll now have a slide presentation by everyone's favorite psychic, Mr. Megadamus!" Lyme announced. "With running commentary on his recent trip to Tangier."

BEYOND THE FAILURE CLUB

The Private expelled a sibilant breath.

"God, this guy's an asshole. Mail frauder, too."

The projection equipment was old, but Megadamus was assisted with it by Miss deHollins, an actress/model who had slipped past her prime before getting her break. Inexpert shots of the Kasbah, a camel market, and such were soon sliding past the eyes of the Failure Club.

"Yes," said Megadamus, "that is your humble psychic with the cobra held 'round his head. Only the force of mental energy prevents the strike of death!"

"Go, snake, go!" The Private muttered.

After the slide show, the members debated whether to support the Fathers' Rights Party on the West Coast. Simon, a would-be opera singer, was for it, while Alain, a meticulous pre-med student, was against. The Private seemed to doze off during the discussion, but he awoke to vote in favor of support. He was on the losing side.

"Lazy bums," he said. "Too much dead wood in here."

Mr. Singh, as Treasurer, gave a rundown on the financial perks of membership. Restaurant coupon books, sports and show passes, group rates on cruises, and discount phone cards were available. The members questioned Singh on the details while The Private smirked sarcastically.

"Can I get a tax write-off on this stuff?" asked Arch, former cult leader convicted of animal abuse.

"Only on part of a part over another part," answered Mr. Singh. "We have group rates so your part comes cheaper than you can buy it. But part of what you pay is over the value of your part, to support our club. Part of this part is tax-deductible depending on how big a part of our income we use on tax-exempt entities. It all depends on our annual financial report." He snickered. "It all comes out in the wash, certified by me." He snickered again.

Arch, heavy-set and unkempt, stared dully from his bird's-nest hair and beard. The meeting soon adjourned.

"How come the VP didn't speak?" Bar asked The Private.

"Judge Waters? He's just window dressing. Senile. Lyme always runs things when Xyntius ain't here."

They were standing amid the folding chairs as members milled about or drifted out the doors. A woman was approaching and Bar recognized her as the one The Private had fondled. She met Bar's eyes with a look of anticipation, eagerness.

"This is Mary Ellen," said The Private. Then, "His name is Bar, short for something else."

"Happy to meet you, Something Else."

"Oh," Bar replied, "no need to be so formal."

They bantered awhile about the meeting.

"You're staying for the campfire, aren't you?"

"There's food and stuff," added The Private. "Beer."

"Well, I didn't bring anything—"

"You can share ours," said Mary Ellen. "You'll be staying overnight, then?"

"Uh, is there a motel around?"

"Fleabag in Argentina," said The Private, "full of welfare bums. Clean our people out hitting them up for handouts."

"Well, I've got a bedroll in the car. Maybe I can rough it on the ground."

"Nah, we can do better than that. Hey, Lyme!"

The chiropractor/secretary turned to them from where he stood chatting.

"Be right back," said The Private. "But hey, Bar, don't get me wrong. You could join us in the mini-camper 'cept, well, you can see we fill it pretty tight."

Mary Ellen reached back with a tight fist, then swung it forward like a club—full force—into The Private's back.

"Oof," he said, and staggered forward, raising his arms. "I surrender. Shit, I surrender!"

He went off laughing to see Lyme. Mary Ellen stood in quiet triumph, as if she'd just made a great tennis serve. She also reminded Bar of a female boxer, light on her feet despite the stockiness.

"Were you in the service, too?" Bar asked.

"No, I'm a nurse. I've been to the places, though. Kosovo, Rwanda, Iraq twice."

"No kidding? That's really something."

"It's with international relief. I've been on call since the first Gulf War."

"Sounds like dangerous work."

"Most of the damage is done before I get there. I help with the burn units mostly, training the local nurses."

"Are you going back anymore?"

She shrugged.

"Where there's a need, I go. That's my life."

The Private was coming back. Bar wondered how Mary Ellen fit into the Failure Club. He noticed that her features looked young, though her brown hair was flecked with gray.

"Cleared it with Lyme," said The Private. "You can pitch your roll in the kitchen annex. He'll leave me the key. Don't tell nobody, though. It's against our contract with the gurus."

They cooked that night next to The Private's truck, which had a tent-like extension on the back. Several other parties had grills going, too, and there was a central campfire, though no one used it for cooking. About half the members had left after the meeting, including the officers. Bar and The Private sat facing the campfire, finishing their burgers, while Mary Ellen approached with a steaming dish.

"Fresh cooked carrots," she offered.

The Private laughed.

"Christ," he said, "Bar ain't one of your aborigines. Take the roots and grubs to Megadamus over there, fatten him up for that cobra."

"How would you like this plate in your face?"

"Hey, I surrendered before, remember? I got rights as a POW."

"Here, I'll try a couple," injected Bar.

She took the rest of the carrots to offer the other campers.

"Never mind us," said The Private. "We got our own way

of relating."

"Nothing like true love."

"Yeah, well, I don't know about that. We lived in the same building, moved in together to save rent."

He laughed.

"See, I was in a garden apartment and she was on the third floor, the top, straight above me. I'd hear her running up the stairs, always running, thumping the stairs. I never seen her so I started thinking, 'There goes Thunderbutt.' The name just came to me. I let it slip when I was talking to the lady on the second floor, in between us. Next thing I know there's this pounding on my door and there's Mary Ellen, giving me hell about calling her Thunderbutt. That's how we met."

"She seems like a really fine person."

"Yeah, she is."

"Hard to figure her belonging to the Failure Club."

The Private grunted.

"Well, you know, you can go around trying to help people, following a call or fighting for a cause, taking orders, and then you come up short on serving your own life. Real short. There's those assholes out there who just want to use you and use you, leave you a shell of what you coulda been, shoulda been. They take all the credit and don't give a damn about you."

"You think they're taking advantage of her?"

The Private gave a start, seemed to refocus.

"Mary Ellen? She's fine. She's okay. Just needs to hold back awhile from self-sacrifice. Christ, she already gave up her childbirth years."

She was smiling coyly when she came back to them, glancing down at the empty plate.

"They ate them all up," she said.

"Megadamus take them all?" chided The Private.

"No, Miss deHollins had some, and Derek, who I know you respect."

"Oh yeah, Derek. Wrote a karate book for the inner city

but couldn't sell any copies. They thought he should give them out free."

He started to laugh but it turned to a cough.

"Fire's getting smoky."

"Bar's going to need the annex opened."

"Uh-oh, there's a hint."

"I guess it's getting kind of late," Bar offered.

"Shit. Well, it's a week night. Guess we can't drop out of society."

The Private led Bar to the small addition on one end of the retreat building. The small space inside was enclosed by kitchen equipment and a closed passage to the main structure.

"Keep the door locked," said The Private. "This is Inner Circle only."

He was closing the door as he said this, so Bar assumed the last reference was a joke. Vague, but they'd each had several beers. He laid out his sleeping bag and turned off the small stove light he'd been using. Lying in the dark, he could gradually make out shapes in the glow from two high windows. He pictured himself at the meeting, zombie-like as the society of losers conducted their ersatz business. Was this where he belonged? Had he sought and reached his natural level? There didn't seem to be much to it, as Ulitreé had said. Not enough. But at least these people faced up to their failures. Dealt with them, sort of. That was better than a lot of others who were just as bad failures, or worse, and just kept kidding themselves. Yeah, Bar thought, I'm a superior sort of failure now. He chuckled as he thought of proclaiming this to Ulitreé.

He was nodding off when there came a scraping sound from the door. Looking over, not fully awake, Bar saw the dim light that meant the door was opening, then a form blocking this light, closing the door on it. Bar remained still and waited.

"I just wanted to check, see you were all right."

"Mary Ellen?"

"Yes."

The door was closing behind her.

"I'm fine, no problem."

He sensed her coming closer.

"Good."

She hesitated.

"We'll be having an early breakfast before we take off. You're welcome to join us if you're up."

"Can't guarantee it, but thanks."

"Well, good night."

"Good night."

She backed to the door and left. She hadn't locked it, but Bar didn't want to get up. Who, he thought, would want to come in here? What was the attraction?

Perhaps five to ten minutes later, Mary Ellen was back. She glided in softly through the unlocked door and was next to Bar before he could think.

"Is it okay if I stay with you awhile?"

"Yeah, sure. But what about—you know, The Private?"

"Asleep, deep REM. Zonked out right after he left you. Well, almost right after."

"Oh."

"You don't have to feel guilty. We never have intercourse. He doesn't want to. Something happened in the service. I just take him orally."

Bar sensed her restlessness.

"My girlfriend and I don't have sex, either. Not even the oral. Her thing, not mine."

Mary Ellen came closer.

"Can I get in there with you?"

He hesitated, knowing he shouldn't but–

"I'll just open it a bit, make more room."

"I'll help you out."

She retreated and began to remove her clothes. Bar unzipped the sleeping bag and laid it out like a blanket. It was still summer, after all, just not real warm. He still had his back to Mary Ellen when she was suddenly next to him.

"Boo," she said.

He viewed her in the faint glow from the windows. Though she'd looked stocky in her clothes, and was in fact large-boned, he saw that she was nicely rounded and proportionate. He stroked her shoulders, then a breast, saw her trim waist and muscular thighs.

"Oh," she said coyly, "you already have an erection," and lightly held the aroused member.

"Yes, nurse."

She leaned forward to kiss him, pushing him back on the bedding. She thrilled at the touch of their bodies, rubbing against him like sandpaper, even their faces. She was strong and aggressive, releasing what had been sealed by The Private's problem. Bar hoped he could hold out but Mary Ellen, as if sensing this, rolled him over on top and clamped her legs behind him. With a shift of her pelvis, she took him within her.

"You can ejaculate any time you want," she said.

Bar tried to delay, raising his torso and pumping, but saw her head turned aside, expectant. Then she was twitching. He released his own sealed passion and was flooded with thoughts of Ulitreé.

It happened once more during the night, longer but less intense, more tender but somehow lacking for it. It was as if a purpose had been achieved. Therapy. They could go on now with the lives that were waiting for them. How trite, some might say. But Bar had no choice. The Private would be waking up and Mary Ellen was gone when dawn entered the windows.

"What's the Inner Circle?" he'd asked after the second time.

"A group, a brotherhood within the club," Mary Ellen replied. "It's secret, but—"

Her voice had fallen to a murmur, trailing off into sleep. Now, hearing faint sounds of activity in the light of day, he was reluctant to join them for breakfast. He'd have trouble facing The Private after what had happened, and he'd put Mary

Ellen in a tough position. So he waited until he heard a vehicle start up and leave, then others. By the time he peeked out the door, The Private's truck was gone and the field was almost empty. He took up his bedroll and exited the annex, leaving the door locked as instructed. He noticed Derek, the inner city karate author, standing nearby and wearing a gie. Derek approached him.

"They're all gone, man. Just me and Collins here."

He was sweating a bit, as if he'd been working out. He nodded toward Collins, former hippie and Air Force schizoid, who sat under a tree reading a book. Collins looked over and smiled.

"Guess I missed breakfast," Bar ventured.

Derek laughed.

"Yeah, I guess you did. But don't worry, man. You'll see them again soon enough."

"The next meeting?"

"You mean *this* bullshit?" A head jerk toward the building. "Hell, no. We don't run this just to hang with silly crybabies!"

He backed away and did a high kick in the air. Bar felt grateful it wasn't in his direction.

"So we're talking, uh, Inner Circle?"

Derek looked amused.

"Yeah, that's good for now. We'll be in touch, man. Phone or email. Don't change your numbers. It won't be here. Something more private."

"But why—how do you know enough about me? This is my first time here."

"Hey, Lyme's the expert on that. All I know is, once you do the Internet form, he finds everything there is on you. Every little fact and figure." A smile. "He probably liked your thing there, too."

He pointed at Bar's amulet, the pentacle engraved on crystal, a gift from Ulitreé. Collins had closed his book and was walking up, his wide, weathered face expressionless.

"So, he with us, then?"

Derek looked irritated.

"Of *course* he's with us. That's why he's here."

"You want change, you got to make it happen," continued Collins. "Can't just wait around for elections, political crumbs. You'll die waiting for crumbs."

Derek nodded assent.

"I take it this involves some risk," said Bar, "maybe—violence?"

"We say sabotage," said Derek.

"Yeah," added Collins, "we're as good as they are with the euphemisms."

"Shit, man," Derek protested.

"Sorry."

Collins dropped his chin and faded back a step. Seems a bit addled, Bar thought, and wondered how far he should go with this.

"We got to get going," said Derek. "We just hung around to give you the word. You know, since The Private had to split."

He pedaled back and did another high kick. Whirling about, he did another, then faced off against an imaginary foe. Collins watched with his thin smile, focused on Derek's forcefulness. Bar sensed this was his cue.

"See you, then," he said to Collins, who did not respond.

"Stay cool!" Derek shouted after him.

They stood and watched as he drove out of the field and down the long gravel drive. He felt some relief as he accelerated on the paved road, but also a new sort of thrill. He was part of something. Not just a bunch of losers fished from the Internet surf, but an elite corps of some sort. He pictured the banner that had hung in the front during the meeting: an orange symbol on purple background, a *V* resting on a line inside a circle. Maybe it was his name, Invictus, that had attracted them. A reminder of their symbol, or of the Inner Circle. But no, there had to be more to it. They weren't just picking him to be a mascot. Anyhow, they must know that he was originally Chester Tracz.

Bar found the highway drive exhilarating, the moving sun confirming the transformation he felt. The night with Mary Ellen after his acceptance by The Private, together with Derek's revelations, met the need that had driven his probing of the Internet. A role—a role in change. It was hard to believe, yet it was happening. Of course, in the back of his mind there were questions about the Inner Circle, the nature and purpose of its "sabotage." But in the bright light of day, the euphoria of personal progress, such doubts were unwelcome intruders.

The change in Bar made a quick impression on Ulitreé. Their laconic, trivial restaurant conversations gave way to searching looks and questions about feelings. She sensed his new strength and wanted to tap into it. They went home to her apartment, then moved to the bedroom at her suggestion. Bar was surprised at first but then saw she wanted the therapy, the strength he'd gained from Mary Ellen and the club.

"We'll do it on a trial basis," said Ulitreé.

With his passion for her partly spent, Bar was able to protract his performance. He arched above Ulitreé as she gazed to one side, concentrating on the feel of his probes. He viewed her blond hair and his saliva on her nipples, reflecting the soft lamplight. Though tall, she seemed delicate after the sturdy Mary Ellen, and Bar recalled his old desire, quickened his thrusts. He felt Ulitreé yield, no longer concentrating, and he again released his passion for her. He collapsed on her, gasping, and they drifted together into sleep.

"I'd like to go next time," she said later, "to the Failure Club. If you're going back, I mean."

"Yeah, I'll probably go. It's about a month till the next full meeting."

"Nothing before then?"

"Not for all the members. Maybe just for the—well, a committee or two, officers and such."

"Okay, I'll go with you next month."

BEYOND THE FAILURE CLUB

Bar was distracted from the club, at first, by the change in Ulitreé. Their entering a full relationship seemed to eclipse the need for other involvements, including the club. But Bar became aware that the club had enabled this change, that it was part of a greater change between him and the world. This showed the potential power and importance of the club—or rather, the Inner Circle. If they wanted him to be part of their group, to help *create* change as well as benefit from it, how could he refuse? They were the matrix of his transformation; his fate and theirs were intertwined. And what greater glories might lie down the road? He sure didn't want to miss out.

As he sat before his computer at Five-County Rehab and Counseling, the dark stillness of the office was eerie to him, rather than the comfort it had been before. The sites he surfed seemed thin, redundant, and his evening passed slowly. But then, as he sat in the glow from the screen, Bar's life turned its critical corner. An email arrived from Dr. Lyme, secretary. Its subject: Breakout Group.

"Glad you'll be joining us, Bar," wrote Lyme. "The others were pretty high on you. Hope you weren't too confused by the shell meeting. Our real people are anything but resigned to failure. As one of them likes to say, we're the 'Talons of the Phoenix.' You'll see for yourself at the conclave. It's Thursday next week, 7:00 p.m."

He gave the address of a restaurant on the way to Chicago.

"We'll be in a private room at the back. Just give my name when you come in. (This info is for 'Talons' only, so write it out and delete this email.) We all look forward to working with you, Bar. We can use your *sang-froid.* Together we'll destroy the vermin in our society and flush them down history's sewers."

Looking away from the screen, Bar sensed the night outside, the endless human activity it contained. No, he was no longer just comforted by the darkness. He was empowered in it. Seclusion had given way to solidarity.

He picked up his pen to copy the restaurant address.

CHAPTER 2

Though most of the students were not yet on campus, Dr. Xyntius was pressed for time. Miss Diaz, his mistress and a department secretary, was furiously typing his syllabi and lecture notes in the next room. This would be their final evening before the return of Mrs. Xyntius, an adjunct instructor, from her summer in New Mexico. Gazing over the campus through his office window, the professor half expected to see his wife arriving early. That would be like her, he thought, demonstrating once again that he'd married a bitch.

Dr. Xyntius was tall, barrel-chested, and bald. He'd been in Michigan for six years now, an associate professor of physics at Horizon State. With the coming year, his service would match what he'd given to Weisbrodt, the selective college in Ohio where he'd met Lauren, his wife. He'd been denied tenure, unfairly he thought, because of their affair while she was a graduate student. It shouldn't matter, he'd argued, because Lauren was in history, not even a physical science, so there was no conflict of interest. They even got married before the tenure decision. Weisbrodt wasn't convinced, however.

They were selective in admitting students and they were selective in granting tenure. He had to leave, and his bright young wife was angered by the loss of security. He quickly became the main target of her complaints.

At Horizon State, there would be no problem with tenure since it didn't exist.

There was also no selectivity. Horizon had been the project of a former governor who thought everyone should get into college, regardless of qualifications. Dr. Xyntius wound up teaching algebra in his physics lectures, restraining clowns in lab sessions, giving multiple choice tests with obvious answers. Lauren, too sour on life to pursue a doctorate, was disgusted nonetheless with the barely literate history students. She therefore took adjunct positions at distant institutions and was gone weeks, even months at a time. At least, thought Dr. Xyntius, they'd avoided the cultural desert of Indiana, whence came his only other offer. But then, that might have pushed Lauren to leave him. Maybe he'd be better off now. Free.

There was a sound from the next room as Miss Diaz swiveled away from her computer. She came into his office with some papers.

"You made a boo-boo, professor."

He loved the lilt in her voice when she teased him.

"Me? A mistake? How dare you!"

"Yes, and not a little mistake. Big time. There's a new chapter in the text, 'Directions for a New Century,' and you have no notes for it. I think that means a low grade for you."

"Come on, Hilda. That's way at the end of the book. I'll be lucky to get halfway through with those characters."

She slowly shook a finger at him, peering up through round-rimmed glasses.

"Now, now. They're your students. Respect is necessary for communication. Remember?"

As always, she amazed him. She remembered everything and insisted on stressing the positive. Of course, she took a dim view of the Failure Club he'd founded, even as he rationalized it. Why not a Success Club? He couldn't convince her that a Failure Club was more apropos for him, something his wife had no trouble recognizing. And, of course, he couldn't let either of them know that the club was a shell for something else—a secret, gathering force that would attack the warped policies in American society. The delicate balance in his life demanded that its people be kept separate, in their places, like the components of an atom or the solar system.

"All right," he said to Hilda. "You're right as usual. Add a sentence that notes for the last chapter will be passed out later."

He watched her return to the other room, envisioned the evening ahead. Only minutes now to their leaving for cocktails, dinner, the night of intimacy in her apartment. In bed she'd call him "my president," referring to his third-party candidacy in a past election. It was his only benefit from the campaign, which hadn't even gained a win over the other third parties. In retrospect, the Relativity Party had simply been incomprehensible to most people. The idea of applying science to social problems and foreign policy called for mental prowess that Americans either didn't have or weren't willing to use. He'd thought it would enhance his career, since the party existed before he joined it, later becoming its candidate. But jousting with lunatics for fifth place had labeled him an eccentric among his peers. To his wife, Lauren, it confirmed that he was failing her. Only with Hilda had it won admiration, gaining him the presidency of their love nest.

Of course, the political scene had also put him in touch with Sokki, his inspiration for the Failure Club—the true, secret leader of the force that was growing within it, an angel of death he'd be seeing very soon.

Sokki had first appeared near the end of the campaign, showing up at meetings, offering the odd suggestion or two. He'd worked a couple of rallies and was there on election night. He seemed a witness more than a participant, devoid of emotional involvement. He stood well over six feet tall, broad-shouldered but gaunt and narrow in the hips. He had whitish hair, wavy and cut short, atop a static pale face with watery gray eyes. His stare was disarming.

"I'll be seeing my friend from Windsor in a few days," Xyntius informed Hilda.

They were having cocktails, safely away from the department offices.

"You'll be going away?"

"To Lansing, yes. We're meeting halfway to share the travel."

"Lauren will be pissed."

"Yes, well, that's too bad. There's the club business to discuss. I'm an academic. I consult others on matters outside my field."

"What kind of business is your friend in?"

"Some kind of landscaper. He sometimes comes over to Detroit on a job, the suburbs mostly."

Hilda gave a coy smile.

"Will you need a secretary there?"

Xyntius looked at her, warmed by the smile. She was small, some would say mousey. Since he himself was bearish, people found them an odd couple. He gave her a return smile, wide and sunny like a salesman's.

"I'd like to need a secretary, but he prefers to meet one-on-one. Then, of course, there's Lauren—"

"She would notice."

"Yes."

They had dinner but didn't linger in the restaurant. Lauren's return lent urgency to their reaching Hilda's apartment and making love. They were quickly in bed, Hilda scrambling with affection over the beached whale that was Xyntius. She was always on top, since he feared crushing her, and they finished with her sitting upright, folding forward during detumescence. He held her against his chest as if she were a child, asleep after story time. So much different than Lauren, Xyntius reflected, though Hilda was just a few years younger. Sex with Lauren brought fussing, demands, complaints. It was an extra relief to finish, to feel her angular form quiet at last beneath him. His secret name for her then was "Rocky Road."

He'd thought about divorce, and could probably do it without financial ruin. Lauren frequently deserted, in a technical sense, so she was at fault, and there was no issue of child support. But there were reasons he needed to keep her that went well beyond the material. Lauren was the sole benefit of his years at Weisbrodt College, for which he'd paid with his position there, his key to a successful career. To give her up now would acknowledge that Weisbrodt had been right in its elitist edict—that he, the son of a warehouse foreman, had no right to be intimate with a daughter of their class. And it would validate the larger class structure, the hidden bigotry based on bloodlines, old money, and secret loyalties. But it wasn't just pride or principle that kept him with Lauren; it was for her sake, too. He was saving her from lapsing into a false identity in her old elitist world. She was unhappy with him, yes, but genuine. He was thus taking a practical stand against the corruption in American society, just as he had with the Relativity Party. He'd gone further there, offering science as an answer to the problem, but people weren't ready for it.

"My president," Hilda said, "run for president again."

"I can't, Miss Diaz. The party fell apart. It's a peace group now."

"Run by yourself. An independent."

"I have something better now. More effective."

"The Failure Club?"

"Yes. Well, some of the people in it, I mean."

She hesitated.

"Am *I* effective?"

He held her in the bed, gave her the sunny smile, watched her warm to it.

"You're indispensable. You're the beauty of life for Jon Xyntius. You inspire me to lead."

She closed her eyes against him, looking more like a child than ever.

...

The drive to Lansing was uneventful, allowing him to mull the feelings he'd had leaving Hilda and Lauren. Like stepping out of water, he thought, one foot from warm and the other from cold. He smiled tightly as he watched the road. He'd like to share that analogy with Sokki, but the Canadian wouldn't react. He'd glance sideways toward nothing in particular, then talk immediately about their business, seeming to be rude. It wasn't his fault, Xyntius knew. He'd been through a lot, had given a lot up.

Sokki was not a native Canadian. He'd moved there to avoid the military draft for the Vietnam War. Though he was covered by the general pardon that came later, he'd never moved back. He'd had a series of mundane jobs and then gone into business for himself. As far as Xyntius knew, Sokki had never married. He wouldn't discuss his relationships, social or political, except for the Failure Club and its nascent inner force. But Sokki had been watching events from afar for a long time, analyzing the developing history of his native country, relating it to his fate and assigning responsibility. He lived now with a mature awareness, unfazed by emotionalism or ideologies. He wasn't looking to get rich, or to gain love or power, but Xyntius sensed he had a goal that was a positive need, perhaps for resolution. The professor felt a flicker of fear when he talked with Sokki.

They met at Dirtbag's Tavern, equidistant from the university and the government buildings. Sokki was waiting for him, seated casually at a table with a stein of dark beer before him. He acknowledged Xyntius with a thin smile, a gentler version of his potent stare. Xyntius ordered a beer.

"Had lunch?" Sokki inquired.

"No."

"We'll order sandwiches when she gets back."

He pulled a menu off the condiment holder and pushed it at Xyntius.

"I already checked it. The brisket sounds good."

Xyntius glanced at the menu and tucked it back. He trusted Sokki's judgment, enjoyed the break from having to use his own. The waitress came and they ordered their sandwiches.

"So," said Sokki, "how are we doing at the Failure Club?"

"No new causes. Members mostly looking for the discounts. Tax return's still delinquent. They don't want to accept Mr. Singh's accounting."

Sokki chuckled, low and confidential.

"I don't blame them."

His smile faded and he glanced slowly around the room.

"And the brothers?" he asked.

"We have a new one, apparently. I'll meet him Thursday at the conclave. He might be just what we wanted—a cooler type, tenacious, to balance out the others."

"What's his name?"

"Byron Invictus. He changed it from something Polish. Dr. Lyme did the full check on him. He's been drifting for quite a while. Never satisfied, smart, the classic loner looking for a cause."

Sokki stared with his watery gray eyes.

"Sounds good. As long as he's solid, we'll move at once on the next project."

Xyntius was taken aback. Their previous project, the burning of a municipal garage, had been practice for something more significant. He hadn't expected it this soon, however. They'd barely settled on who was in their operating group.

"The brothers—they want a name to operate under. They're suggesting 'Talons of the Phoenix.'"

Sokki looked away, reflecting.

"Sounds kind of video-game. I'd have opted for something more subtle, sophisticated. But the point is to be effective. If it helps them do the work, let them have the name they want.

'Talons' it is."

The waitress brought their sandwiches. They ate for a while, but the unresolved question of the new project hung between them. Though the tension surrounding the first project was still fresh in his mind, Xyntius wanted to show solidarity. So he returned to the subject himself, asking Sokki what he was planning.

"Well, first of all, let's be clear with each other that we want to go ahead. We can minimize our risks, but there can be unintended results. It'll get more likely as we go up the ladder. Are you ready to accept that, so we can achieve our purpose?"

"Of course," Xyntius replied.

The promptness of his answer seemed to surprise Sokki. But the challenge had brought Hilda to mind for Xyntius, as if *she* were asking the question, testing her president.

"All right, then," Sokki continued. He glanced around and spoke softly. "This is still developmental, but we want to step up to explosives and a more substantial target. Government, of course."

"Still the no-casualty rule?"

"Absolutely. We're not killers, unlike them. That has to be understood, has to be our message."

"Agreed. And the target, this more substantial one?"

"A rest stop on one of the interstates."

Xyntius took a moment to absorb this, verify that Sokki was serious. But then, he was always serious. He was dead set on it, in fact. It was the product of many years of lonely deliberation. So there was no reason to laugh, or even to question very far.

"It would have to be empty, not in use. Is one of them closed?"

"I don't know. But it doesn't matter because we're going for one that's business as usual. Except we'll hit it when there's no one in it. Middle of the night, early morning."

"But the traffic going by is constant. There's no way to be sure—"

"That's where your new guy comes in, the new 'Talon.' We need someone with ice in his veins sitting right in front of the facility, after it's been rigged, to give the word on when to detonate."

"The actual bombers are somewhere else?"

"They're at the rest stop on the other side of the interstate, for traffic going the other way. They detonate by remote control."

"What about Byron, sitting right in front?"

"He gets ten seconds after giving the word. So he has to be on his way out when he gives the go."

"That's cutting it pretty close."

"Has to be, so no one goes in after he leaves."

"Understood. But can't they just watch through binoculars for when it's clear?"

"Too chancy. There's trees, traffic in the way. And we don't know what the weather will be like. Plus, we want the option of checking inside in case there's any doubt."

Xyntius looked away, visualizing the scene. He would have to sell this to the Talons at their conclave. Some would be eager to proceed, but one or two might have doubts, as he himself vaguely did.

"What about expertise?"

"Well, on the programming we have Dr. Lyme, plus Collins with his Air Force training. You yourself can determine the charge we need. Let The Private get the explosives through his old contacts. Use as many lookouts as possible during the rigging, so we can work calmly, safely."

"How many charges?"

"That's up to you. But, of course, we *do* want to send a message. We can't have them thinking it was just an accident, fireworks or something."

"Agreed."

They talked awhile about parts, Sokki saying he could bring them in with his equipment if necessary. But Xyntius knew he could get what they needed from the labs at the university, so it seemed they were ready to go ahead. They finished their lunch and Sokki suggested they have a stroll.

"There's a small arboretum nearby," he said. "Professional interest."

As they walked, Sokki seemed aloof from his surroundings, his long legs striding at a relaxed pace. He gazed into the farthest distance, expressionless. The traffic beside them was heavy and noisy.

"Unlimited production of cars, other vehicles," Sokki said. "Funny we haven't reached permanent gridlock."

"Well," said Xyntius, "there's planned obsolescence."

Sokki laughed.

"Our savior. Obsolescence as value. Tells you who's in charge, doesn't it?"

"Yes, unfortunately."

"The bottom-liners. Sitting at the top with society all set up for them. White House on down."

"People buy into it, though. The products, the wars. Agree with the corporate line or you're not patriotic. Life is now a string of banal, short-term goals for which people give up their dignity, and other people's. Obey the boss, adore the flag, kill the designated enemy."

"An old problem, though, Vietnam and before. The 'Greatest Generation,' greatest at needing enemies and sending young guys to kill or be killed. They had to keep feeling like heroes after Hitler was gone, no matter how much death and ruin they caused."

"Well, there was no real culture to fall back on. What do we have in comparison with the old cultures of Europe and Asia? Their achievements in art, literature, and science over the ages? We make the most bombs, justify their use on TV, treat them as toys in video games. That's our culture."

"Yeah," said Sokki. "That's why it's fair game."

They came to the arboretum, an oasis of vegetation amid the bustle of the state capital. Xyntius waited respectfully as Sokki examined plants, then sat with him on a bench. Staff and clients from the government buildings strolled past them.

"So, here we are," said Xyntius, "relaxing with the two-party system."

"Well, why not? Doesn't it belong in the Failure Club?"

"Certainly. If only more people could see it—"

"They won't as long as they see two parties, instead of the *one* that's really there."

"That single corporate agenda, rumbling along unopposed. The smokescreen of red herring issues."

"The Republicans are best at that. But I blame the Democrats more. The constant selling out, being absorbed into the imperial program."

"Yet they still give the illusion of representing the masses, thus cutting off any third-party momentum."

"The masses. Yeah, with their fears and bigotry ready to be exploited by the Republicans—the media and the Democrats falling in line. Return the plan for empire to another term."

"Well, the media is corporate turf. Progressives are shut out and, with the collapse of the Democrats, disenfranchised."

Sokki looked in his eyes.

"And, at the core?"

"The core?"

"The core of the progressives."

"Oh. Well, alienated, I suppose."

Sokki looked back to the bureaucrats. Xyntius sensed an icy confidence building.

"There are some smart people in those movements," Sokki said, "but it isn't enough just to be right. You also have to make an impact. Do some damage. The big boys just laugh at demonstrations, petitions, et cetera."

"As the old tycoons laughed at the early unions. They would tolerate no rules in amassing their wealth."

"Those bastards. They even wanted colonies, didn't they? The Spanish-American War?"

"A set-up, yes. And now we've come full circle. The

mentality is back in force. Today Iraq, tomorrow the world."

"Which is where *we* come in."

"Sabotage."

"Yeah," Sokki smiled, "sabotage."

• • •

The red digits on the motel alarm clock read 2:48. Xyntius had been sleeping, but was awakened by a dream of toilets exploding. The new project, of course. Apparently there was an unresolved issue in the deeper recesses of his psyche. He had full confidence in Sokki, depended on him for originality and timing in their planning, so the question, he thought, must involve his own role. Was there something inappropriate, something he was doing wrong? He was deceptive, he knew, toward the university, Lauren, and most of the Failure Club. But secrecy was natural and necessary in the work they were doing. What might not be necessary, though, thinking of Lauren, was his stubborn retention of his marriage to her.

In foregoing divorce, Xyntius wondered, was he still aspiring to the elite that had spawned his wife? Did he continue to claim a role in the corporate hegemony that he and Sokki were planning to destroy? The status he'd sought was surely a form of obeisance to the enemy, helping to perpetuate its power in concert with corrupt or spineless politicians. Accepting or wanting a high place in the class structure was to endorse the values and policies that gave it strength. But he was opposed to those things. Together with Sokki, he was their sworn enemy.

He grabbed the phone and dialed Hilda's apartment. After half a dozen rings, he heard her groggy "hello."

"I've decided to get a divorce," he told her.

"A divorce?"

"Yes."

"You decided now, in the middle of the night?"

"Yes, it became clear to me."

"Maybe it would be more clear in the daytime, after you have coffee. In your professor suit."

"It's not like that, Hilda. It isn't a physics problem. Not in the academic sense, anyway."

"Jon, my president. You're so funny. Sweet and funny. But, you know, you don't have to marry me for me to love you. You have your career, your other work, all so important. To me, also. Too much to risk, to lose, to do that divorce business."

Xyntius hesitated. Maybe he'd missed something, as he often did in papers he gave her to process.

"Risk, you say? I don't know that I see it."

"We have our love, Jon, and your life with Lauren goes along. It's stable. The divorce would shake it up, make it a storm—make your whole life stormy. How could our love find its way, not be bothered? We need to keep our peace, our day-to-day protected, so we can keep our room to love, our private times."

Xyntius had no response. He'd assumed she wanted more eventually. Instead, she gave new cause to stay with Lauren.

"Jon? Hello?"

"Yes, I'm here. Maybe you're right. I'll have to rethink it. Sorry I woke you up, Hilda."

"Yes, you should be. But it's okay, I always like to talk to you. You'll be in for the afternoon? There might be students needing permissions, lacking prerequisites."

"Yes, tell them one o'clock. I might be earlier—*probably* will. Won't stay long at the house."

"Lauren."

"Yes."

After they'd hung up, Xyntius slept soundly with no more visions of exploding toilets. Even when he woke, his thoughts of the project were fleeting since he preferred to think of Hilda. Once on the road, though, the hard feel of asphalt drove home the purpose of this trip—the next extralegal move for progress by Sokki and himself. His mentor seemed confident, but to

Xyntius the execution of their plan seemed complicated and too visible. They had to be undetected, to make gains without losing anything, especially their anonymity. He'd have to stress this at the conclave, ensure that the Talons functioned smoothly as a unit, each of them in the role best suited to his or her skills.

He sighted a place called The Pottery Barn down the road. He'd seen it on the way in, a shed near a farmhouse with homemade signs and a couple of giant urns on display. He'd resolved to stop on his way back and pick something up for Hilda, perhaps also for Lauren. A woman came out from the farmhouse when Xyntius pulled into the yard. He selected two small vases in the natural clay color, each with a few lateral stripes painted in black. On one the stripes were thick and moved sharply up and down, a series of sharp points around the vase. On the other the stripes were thinner and undulated in rounded waves. At first he thought the vase with points would be for Lauren, its pattern suggesting her volatility, heat. The waves on the other could stand for the tranquility he found in Hilda. But then he saw that it was Hilda who, for him, provided heat and the energy to surge forward with confidence. Lauren was remote from him, though they lived together, and separated by cool waves of indifference.

Back on the road, Xyntius reflected on how the most meaningful parts of his life—the Talons and Hilda—were both secret. His marriage to Lauren, his PhD, and his ersatz career were mere covers, just as the Failure Club was a shell group for the Talons. He hadn't controlled the events that brought this about, but he believed it was right.

"In secrecy there is meaning," he said to himself.

CHAPTER 3

Through the late September haze, two rest areas faced each other across the interstate, one of them rigged with bombs. It was 4:15 a.m., and four men sat in a minivan at the non-rigged facility. They had placed the charges, three in number, and were waiting for a signal to detonate by remote control. Their colleague, who would give the signal, was alone in his car in front of the other facility. He'd wait until the building was empty, since there were to be no casualties, and until he could escape unseen. The men in the van would escape in the opposite direction as soon as one of them, The Private, had pushed the buttons to detonate. The senior member of the crew, he was stocky with tousled dark curls and tinted glasses.

"Should I have the motor running?" asked Andrew, the driver.

"Nah," The Private replied. "We don't want no attention."

"Any chance they won't go off?" asked Derek, who sat behind them.

"They'll go," said The Private. "Everything was placed and set according to specs. Right, Collins?"

"Yo!" came a voice from the back, where Collins lay in apparent boredom. His anxious companions weren't surprised by this, since Collins had been discharged from the Air Force as a schizoid. He was gangly with longish hair.

"At least you guys are more used to this," said Andrew. "I was pretty much numb as a lookout. How about you, Derek?"

"Damn right, man."

"Well, the plan said lookouts, maximum caution," said The Private. "It wasn't no picnic for us, either. Or for Bar, sitting over there hoping we don't hit the buttons early."

"I can dig *that*," said Derek. He nodded for emphasis, his eyes intense beneath his short Afro.

They were the Talons of the Phoenix, a secret inner circle of the Failure Club, a social organization for losers that recruited via the Internet. The Talons were culled from the hapless general membership by leaders who were not at the rest stops this night, but who managed the bombing from afar. It was developmental, to prepare the Talons for greater acts of sabotage against corrupt government and the corporate kingpins it served. Two months before, a municipal garage had been burned in Ohio. Tonight, in Indiana, a highway rest stop would fall victim to the cause. For the Talons, it was a step up. They were advancing toward victory over a hidden enemy that controlled society and plundered the world.

"We got our time window yet?" yawned Collins.

"Yeah," The Private answered. "Trooper went through eight, nine minutes ago. Won't be back for more'n a hour. Coffee stop and shit."

"We're just waiting on Bar, then," said Derek.

"Right."

Behind the wheel, Andrew stared in the direction of the other rest stop and wondered how his counterpart was doing. Bar had apparently been chosen because he was used to working alone and at night, and because of his steady nerves. As for himself, Andrew had no illusions. He was driving the van for his clean record in case they were stopped. Somewhat younger than his companions, Andrew was clean-shaven with light brown hair. He was a school counselor, stuck in the job due to his specialized degree. He'd been highly satisfied at first, but he came to see that his influence on people was minimal in the face of class structure and deteriorating culture. He was ineffective due to the system and the amoral materialists who controlled it.

"This guy Bar is a social worker?" he asked The Private.

"Case manager. Don't have your hundred-proof degree."

Andrew knew the type. They'd entered the social services before the MSW was necessary, then couldn't get anywhere for the lack of it. So they floated from job to job, trying to make up in variety what they lacked in promotions and professional respect. Still, Bar and he were colleagues in a way, and doubly so since they were fellow Talons. Together they were violating their role in society, that of official bleeding hearts, to engage in what would be seen as domestic terrorism. What was not seen, of course, was the corruption they were fighting in order to *save* society, and perhaps civilization.

"What's keeping him?" Derek wondered. "Nothing's been coming off the ramp. Those truckers got to be asleep."

"Maybe one of them ain't," said The Private. "Got the runs or something. Anyway, we got no choice. We gotta wait. If I ring him, I might miss his signal."

Derek sighed heavily. He wasn't into weapons, Andrew knew, but was an expert in karate, on which he'd written an unsuccessful book. Derek lived and worked in the inner city, which Andrew saw as two strikes against *any* sort of success. He'd seen it up close doing field work for his degree. He'd been impressed by the lack of progress from conditions of the '60s, as they were widely chronicled. He hadn't returned to work there after graduation, but the experience reinforced his antipathy toward the controllers of wealth and social institutions. Gazing across the interstate, Andrew wondered about his colleague, the case manager. Had Bar's disillusionment been similar, even without the MSW? Maybe they could get together later and share insights, discuss why two do-gooders like themselves were taking part in planned violence.

• • •

Across the highway, Byron Invictus sat alone before the bomb-rigged building. His was the only car, but there were three trucks with trailers parked in the separate lot behind him. Two were facing the building while the third was parked askew farther back in the lot. Byron, known as Bar to his fellow Talons, had rather shaggy, dark-blond hair and rimless glasses. He was concerned about the third truck, positioned as it was for a quicker exit. Bar knew that the rest facility was empty, so it was only his need for escape that delayed his detonation call. No casualties and no detection: that was the order. Knowing the window of opportunity was limited, Bar hurried to calculate his jump on the third truck, how long to the next exit, whether he could evade within the speed limit.

Almost a full day before, and half a state away, Bar had rolled out of the bed he shared with Ulitreé. Their relationship had been non-sexual until he'd joined the Failure Club and been admitted to its secret core, the Talons of the Phoenix. The sense of belonging and confidence he'd gained from the Talons were things he'd never known before, either as an ethnic type in Chicago or as the drifter he became. Ulitreé had quickly sensed his new confidence and drew her own from it, so their relationship was finally complete. She'd come to the next general meeting of the Failure Club, but was unaware of the Talons, as were most of the club members. Yet they served as a convenient shell and pool for recruitment, a setup that earned Bar's respect for the shadowy leadership.

He had to make a move, Bar thought. Now. Before another car stopped and the time window closed.

He turned in his seat. Beyond the two sleepers, the third truck sat poised for pursuit. But Bar sensed he had his edge. The trucker had no idea what was happening, would be distracted by the explosions, perhaps blocked by smoke.

Bar dialed the number to give the "all clear," but didn't press the *send* button yet. Instead, he quietly started the car and backed out of the parking space. As he idled toward the exit, he pressed *send* and The Private's phone rang in the opposite rest area across the interstate.

"Counting ten," came The Private's voice.

"Counting nine," Bar responded.

"Counting eight," said The Private.

And that was all. Phone on the seat beside him, Bar was flooring the gas and rocketing onto the almost empty highway. He heard the charges go like a nearby thunderclap that shattered the hazy country night. He glanced in the rear-view and saw no lights behind him. Distant taillights appeared up ahead and Bar eased on the gas, found the other car was moving ten over the speed limit. He wouldn't pass, would stay undetected. He dropped to five over the limit. Let the other guy be trooper bait; he himself had commitments, reasons to be careful and obey the law. He knew the irony but wouldn't laugh. He'd be dead serious till he'd seen this through all the way. It meant that much to him.

Bar got off at the first available exit. There were some businesses near the ramp, but they were closed because of the hour. He pulled into a restaurant lot, extinguished his lights, and sat staring at the interstate. A car shot by, then a truck, and gradually his heart stopped pounding. His mind was in a whirl, nothing clear as to what he should do next. He could reverse course on the interstate, passing the sabotage, and join the other Talons at their motel. Or he could continue on to Indy, swing north, and head for home and Ulitreé. The second option became more inviting as he reflected on what they had done. Domestic terrorism. An act that would earn them harsh punishment and permanent infamy if they were caught. He'd done it for his brother Talons to earn his place among them, and he'd swing with them if it came to that. He needed to belong, and to something great. But for tonight his heart and mind had been ravaged, unexpectedly, by the intensity of the execution of their plan. He reached for his phone to call Dr. Lyme, secretary of the Failure Club, who was waiting at the designated motel.

"No bird dogs," he said when Lyme answered.

"Gotcha," answered the secretary. "Coming to prayer meeting?"

"Pass. Need some home cooking."

"I'll tell the choir. Take care."

"Right. Disconnect."

"Disconnect."

Bar took a deep breath and started his car. He had to move on before he was noticed. Back on the road, he felt secure in his achievement and escape. Sure, it was a serious thing they'd done, but the Talons had their positive purpose, something he accepted. And it was by far the biggest *thrill* of his life. That's why it had rattled him for a while. He'd moved up another level, another step toward greatness from the sappy banality he'd known before.

You have to break a few eggs, he thought.

• • •

After the detonation, Andrew had pulled out of the opposite rest area as casually as he could. The others in the van, his fellow Talons, were scrambling around in their excitement, Collins straining for looks out the windows while Derek and The Private exchanged hand slaps, shakes, and bumps. It was the sudden relief from tension and the thrill of victory. There was still an edge of fear, but their confidence was mounting to meet it. Andrew shared their emotions but also knew his job and struggled to do it, fighting the impulse to floor the gas pedal or lean on the horn.

"Seatbelts, please! State law!" he shouted.

"Shit, yeah," said The Private. "We don't wanna blow it *now*. Get your seat belt, Derek. You too, Collins."

Collins continued to paw the windows, oblivious.

"Hey Collins, what the fuck! Swat him, Derek."

They secured the errant member and coasted along the highway toward their rendezvous with Dr. Lyme. The traffic was lighter than ever, vehicles apparently slowing to view the sabotage. The Private pulled himself together and punched in Dr. Lyme's phone number.

"Confirm delivery," he said. "Carrier en route. Disconnect."

"Hoo-ee!" Derek kept saying. "Did you see that sucker *blow*!"

Collins was laughing.

"Man, that was—I don't know, that was like God, you know? Like God back there."

"I don't know about no God, man. That was a *statement*, man. Loud and clear. As loud and clear as it's ever gonna get!"

"Wow, yeah. Great."

"Damn right it's great. Let the fat cats, the crooks at the top—all of them—sit up and take notice. Here's what you got coming, suckers!"

The Private was sobering, peering down the road.

"You know the exit?"

"Sure," Andrew replied. "Second one, then north a ways."

"Good. No offense, just staying organized." Then, to Derek, "I dunno. Thought I heard a extra burst. Four, not three. They had a little drum, tank or something, near the building. Mighta been gas, oil. Mighta made a extra blast."

"Well, good. More power to us, man."

"Maybe not. We don't know what it done. We got to be precise. Just do the damage in the plan. We're on a long-range program. These guys know what they're doing, but it gotta go down exactly."

"So tell Lyme about it. But we're outta there, man. We did our job."

The Private looked back to the road.

"Right. We're outta there."

Andrew drove silently, passed the first exit. Since he lived in Wisconsin, he tended to miss meetings and didn't know his companions well. He admired their dedication, though, thinking it might be purer than his own. They didn't have his graduate education, yet they instinctively saw through the cultural program imposed on them: the lotteries, sports rituals, "reality" shows, conformist music, news requiring nationalism. It all tended to defuse or distract from controversy, or to soften people up for changes in popular thinking: it's okay now to torture, imprison without trial, assassinate. One TV drama had won repeated awards as it promoted these practices. The government could thus rule through fear on behalf of its corporate sponsors, while a majority of Americans were conditioned by their culture to accept it.

"Almost there," said The Private, spotting their exit sign.

He has someone waiting for him, Andrew reflected. The Private's girlfriend, Mary Ellen, had remained at the motel with Dr. Lyme. She was a nurse and the only female Talon, a detail that called for improvement. Andrew had someone waiting for him, too—his legal wife. But she was at their home in Wisconsin, far from the present scene, so Andrew would have to wind down on his own. He'd think of his wife increasingly as he finished up with the Talons, picture her with their baby daughter in the small house outside Madison. They were as sheltered and secure as possible against a society stirred by hate and arrogance, religious and national fanaticism. It helped to have the buffer of the university community, though Andrew didn't consider himself a "liberal." He was simply committed to what made sense, what seemed necessary for his daughter as he watched her in her crib. He expressed this commitment in his work with the Talons. He knew he had a lot to lose, but he made this his reason to do things right.

They reached the exit and Andrew pulled off the interstate toward the motel. It was a cheap one with the rooms opening directly to the outdoors. No lobby or hallway meant less chance of detection, Dr. Lyme had reasoned. He was waiting with Mary Ellen when the van arrived, Andrew parking it several rooms away. They entered in pairs, Andrew and Derek following five minutes after The Private and Collins. When Andrew went in, The Private was in quiet conversation with Mary Ellen, who was also stocky and had salt-and-pepper hair. Collins was getting a spinal adjustment from Dr. Lyme, a practicing chiropractor.

"Great work, men," said Lyme. "Anyone else want to celebrate with a free adjustment?"

"No thanks, Doc," Derek replied. "Me and your patient will celebrate with something else when you're done beating him up."

"How about you, Andrew?"

"No, sir. I'm fine."

"Well, that should hold for now, Collins. Guess you have a bottle or something waiting. Be sure and watch the noise, now. It was a big night for us, a victory, but we have to keep it in the family. We can't afford any public announcements."

"We know the drill," said Derek. "Come on, man. Time to change rooms."

Having regained his edgy composure, Derek led Collins out the door. The night's work was its own reward for him, Andrew knew, as it was for all of them. No mercenaries in the Talons of the Phoenix. The Private and Mary Ellen were moving to leave, too, the nurse beaming with infinite relief.

"Just one thing, Doc," said The Private. "The boom, it sounded like four beats, not three. That little tank near the building—silver, hot-dog shaped—we mighta got some extra bang there."

A shadow of concern passed over Dr. Lyme's face. He

quickly recovered, however, giving a professional smile that complemented his styled hair, goatee, and designer glasses.

"Not to worry," he said. "We had Byron there giving the 'all clear.' No one closer than the truck and trailer lot. Even if there's toxic residue, they'll catch it in the response. No sweat, my man!"

"Yeah, right. Just thought I'd let you know."

The Private left with Mary Ellen. Andrew was left with Dr. Lyme, the room suddenly dull, predictable, with just the two of them in it. Andrew admired Lyme's organizational and technical skills, but he didn't identify with Lyme's flamboyant, sometimes careless style. He wished that Dr. Xyntius, the Failure Club president and head of the Talons, would take a greater part in supervising operations. The reserved professor of physics, Andrew thought, would give steadier, more professional leadership than the jack-of-all-trades chiropractor. He wouldn't have to worry so much about his rambunctious comrades. Maybe Bar, the new guy, would be a help in that area—moral and intellectual ballast in the storm of emotions around them.

"So," Lyme said, "long night."

"That's for sure. But fruitful."

"Yes, you can all be proud. I'm sure Dr. Xyntius will be pleased. And now, guess you're itching to get back to the family. I know *I* am."

Like Andrew, Lyme was married and a parent. His children numbered two, however, and they were school-age. Andrew was conscious of being junior to Lyme, in age and otherwise. This, together with their differences in style, made their relating awkward.

"Right," Andrew answered. "By the way, did Bar make it back? Byron?"

"No. He called, though. Said everything was fine on his end. Decided to head straight home to his lady friend. Can't blame him."

"She's in the club, isn't she?"

"The shell, yeah."

"I thought I might see him here, compare notes. We work in the same field, more or less."

Lyme looked at him, surprised by something.

"You and Bar? Yeah, I guess so. Only, I think Bar might've taken a different way here than you and me. No steady career path. He's bounced around a lot. I don't know that I'd expect much from him as to professional insights."

"But he saw enough to join the Talons, to contribute."

"He's in, yes, and he's valuable. And there's no question of his dedication. But I see him strictly as a *performer* for us. Nothing on the theory side, the planning."

"And I'm different that way?"

Lyme smiled.

"Patience, my son. We have a lot ahead of us. We'll be looking to widen our scope, and the *scale* of our operations. Get beyond the Midwest, go for higher-level targets. I expect we'll be adding operatives. There should be a leadership role for you."

His hard look converted it to a promise. As long as I stay a good soldier, Andrew thought.

"These new operatives, you're thinking they'll come from the Failure Club?"

Dr. Lyme chuckled.

"I'll admit the current pool isn't promising. But we have our national membership, even *inter*national, that participate through the Internet. They're not at the meetings because of the distance. Then, too, Dr. Xyntius has other sources."

"What about intelligence?"

"IQ or CIA? Don't answer—we got'em both."

Andrew only nodded. He was feeling some satisfaction from this camaraderie—not with Dr. Lyme as a person, but with his leadership.

"What the hell," Lyme continued. "As of tonight, consider yourself up half a notch. A field promotion. Same standing as

The Private, only he's strictly operations. You're in with us cerebral types."

Andrew's satisfaction deepened.

"Thanks. I suppose this doesn't extend to planning, major decisions?"

"Hey, there are different levels but even I'm just a foot-soldier, basically. Oh, Dr. Xyntius is open to suggestions, but the projects are *his* babies, though he might have a confidante or two."

"Yes, I've heard there was someone else. Just a rumor."

"Well, we don't have to worry about it—where they rank with us, I mean. We don't worry that much about ranks. Don't need'em in the Talons. Everything is based on trust, our common purpose. The Failure Club is something else. Bullcrap. A good shell organization, but bullcrap. So we have titles to keep it organized, just like in the larger bullcrap society, where nothing is based on trust. Can't be. Too many crooks protected by the system."

Andrew was nodding again.

"Okay," said Lyme, "I'll get off my soapbox. I know you're tired. So am I. I'm glad we had this talk, Andrew. I feel we accomplished something."

"So do I, sir. And you have my word I'll do everything I can for the Talons."

Dr. Lyme offered his hand. Andrew reached into the viselike grip.

• • •

Bar felt a lot better with a burger and coffee in him. He'd found a restaurant open near one of the Indy exits, considered eating inside. The place was clean, well-lit, a pleasing contrast to his dark adventure. But he was supposed to minimize visibility. So he ate in his car, alone again in the dark. Now, as he cruised northward through the heart of the state, he thought about calling Ulitreé. But he wasn't sure she'd be up yet, and he wasn't ready to answer questions about his night's activities. He'd gained hugely in confidence with her, gone from sexless to sensual, but there *was* this one secret between them, the secret of the Talons. It would be a challenge for him to protect it, but he had no choice. He depended on the Talons for his self-worth, his confidence, his attractiveness to Ulitreé. Without the Talons, he'd collapse into the social garbage he'd been before.

Bar flicked on the radio, scanned the frequencies for some talking.

"We're very fortunate," came a stolid male voice, "that no one was in the building at the time, or close to it. We could've been dealing with fatalities here, or much more serious injuries."

"Any leads at this point?" asked the female reporter.

"Well, there's obvious suspicious circumstances," said the policeman. "We'll be doing a thorough investigation as the wreckage cools. We'll try to recover the surveillance tapes, but it's doubtful they're in usable condition."

"Thank you, sergeant. The public is asked to contact the state police or local law enforcement with any information you may have on this catastrophe. Your identity will be protected."

She signed off to the studio, where a male colleague finished up.

"The truck driver whose windshield shattered is expected to be released following treatment for his cuts and a precautionary x-ray."

"Shit," Bar muttered.

They'd drawn blood, something they definitely wanted to avoid. It was part of their philosophy as he understood it: property damage only. Now, this blot on their record—on his debut with the Talons. Maybe the windshield had been cracked, or defective. Could it be established somehow? Christ, he thought, I'm really reaching.

He switched the radio to music.

Thing is, Bar considered, you have to expect some people are going to get hurt. There can't be surgical precision when you're using bombs, fire, and such. No more for the Talons than for our military going into Afghanistan, Iraq, et cetera. Even less for the Talons, since we have to worry about avoiding detection, getting away unseen. Of course, guns would be more exact—rifles, not handguns. If people are going to get hurt anyway, why not put it directly to the assholes you're after? Why should that trucker take the flak that our social vermin deserve? But the guys in charge don't want to do it just now, so I'd better keep this to myself. When they change their minds, though—*if* they change them, I'm ready to go. Fire away, Gridley. Blow those suckers to hell.

He was still driving as dawn began to break, reminding him of Ulitreé in the glory of their bed. His skin recalled the textures of her body and it irked him that he had to wait for her. Her day shift, his evening shift, then finally as midnight approached he could lose himself in her. Except for his status as a Talon, of course—the part of Byron Invictus on which all else depended. That must always persevere, be foremost in his consciousness. The Talons were his life, so he'd do whatever they asked of him.

CHAPTER 4

As he stood at his living-room window, Sokki could view the skylines of both Windsor and Detroit, the twin upper edges of his dual citizenship. He was perhaps six-three, but hadn't been measured since his physical for the Vietnam War, which he'd avoided by moving to Canada. He could have returned with the general pardon, but there was a lack of sympathy for it in his old Kansas community. Besides, he was doing all right in his new home, he'd made friends, and he savored his freedom from a warrior country's patriotism. He was still interested in the United States, of course, and watched its developments closely from his perch on the border. There was an ember of resentment in him, deep and long denied, that was glowing hotter now as he approached retirement age. It yearned to dispel the notions of how his life might have gone if it hadn't been disrupted. Failing this, it would seek a different finality, a fiery consummation only temporarily delayed by other fulfillments.

Behind him, the afternoon sun stretched his shadow, broad-shouldered but gaunt, through his spacious living room. The furniture was Scandinavian in style, since Sokki detested the heavy dowdiness of his upbringing. In art, his taste ran to nudes, though he'd lately drifted from paintings to photography. A huge reproduction of Modigliani's mistress, by Rudomine, graced the wall above his main couch. This was a source of irritation for Alypia, who was visiting that day from Montreal, since she felt it distracted from political discussion. But Sokki had lost his taste for interpretations and the abstract, was interested now only in the literal, cutting through the chaff. Alypia, or Lyp as he called her, could appreciate this, but she clung to the forms of their old discussion group, where they'd been at opposite ends of the age spectrum. Sokki, of course, was the elder.

Beyond the living room, Sokki's kitchen was hung with copper cooking utensils and fine cutlery, virtually unused. He never cooked, but enjoyed the ambience of reddish metallic glows and potent glints. Lyp might use the kitchen to make pasta during her stay, but they'd have to shop for the makings. Sokki was well stocked with breads and wines, deli meats, and vegetables, but little else. He kept his diet simple but free from dogma, as he thought everything should be. Lyp wasn't quite in agreement, having worked with the separatist movement when very young, but she was coming around to his view that flexibility helped maintain focus. Too many rules or ideals were a fatal hindrance to success, the achievement of your one most vital purpose.

Walking through the apartment, Sokki glanced into the bedroom used as a bedroom, as opposed to the one that had other purposes. Everything was in order for Lyp. The leopard-skin cover on the king bed complemented his wooden masks from Africa and New Guinea. He'd screwed the mirror back onto the bureau so Lyp could use it while dressing. It was normally down and facing the wall, Sokki sparing himself the daily forced view of his disarrayed aging. The stare of his watery gray eyes from his pale face, disarming to most people, was something even *he* had to take in degrees. He kept his whitish, wavy hair cut short to lessen the effect, but he wasn't really sorry that he bothered people. It was a convenient preemptive strike, after all—a warning not to pull anything on him. They were dealing with an unknown quantity, capable perhaps of violent retribution.

The other bedroom contained Sokki's computer, top of the line with the latest upgrades and maximum armor against viruses and hackers. In a nearby corner were stacks of books, magazines, newsletters, and printouts from around the world. A compact shredder lurked in another corner. On the wall next to the door was a world map, illuminated by diffuse sunlight from the windows opposite. The wall to the computer's right contained a triangular display of mug shots clipped from publications or computer output. There were about forty of these photos, including some of well-known officials and a couple with *Xs* drawn through them. This would have been the room's compelling feature were it not for the use to which Sokki had put the opposite wall. There, pinned to specially-installed cork paneling, was a vast montage of materials he'd collected over the past several decades.

Toward the upper left corner were headlines, photos, and articles concerning President Kennedy's assassination. Pictured were the figures involved or later implicated, with the CIA agents phasing into the center third of the wall, which was headed by stories on the Bay of Pigs invasion and CIA resentment of JFK's lack of support. Close below were stories about his plans to reduce CIA power. The right side of the wall began with the fall of the Diem regime in Vietnam, shortly before Kennedy's death, and the cancellation of his pullout plans by Lyndon Johnson. Below the assassination stories on the left of the wall were the many criticisms of the Warren Report, with postmortem photos, charts of shooting angles, analyses of Oswald's contacts and his weapon. Next to these articles, in the CIA column, were stories of mind-control experiments, a school of torture, the overthrow of Allende, and a supposed cleanup of the agency in 1976. The Vietnam column reflected the sorry history of that war, including the bombing of Cambodia and its aftermath.

On the lower portion of the wall, the three columns tended to dovetail. Congress admitted there was a JFK conspiracy and the CIA was implicated when E. H. Hunt lost a slander suit. Biological weapons were being sold to Iraq, closely followed by the Iran-contra affair, and then the Gulf War. Global business interests grew along with various espionage and military adventures. Following "9-11" came the second Iraq war, and Sokki's articles listed the flaws in its rationale. Profits in oil and war supplies were researched, along with corporate control of the media and the influence of financiers on government. At the bottom of the wall was a banner that Alypia had sewn. On a green field were blood-red letters reading "CORPORATE HEGEMONY." Someone had drawn an arrow from the banner to an article on Permindex, the elite business group connected to JFK's assassination. It was one of his visitors, Sokki would say. He himself needed no arrows to see the connections here.

Seated now at his computer, Sokki accessed the site of the Failure Club, a social organization for losers that recruited via the Internet. It contained a secret inner circle of social militants, the Talons of the Phoenix. While Sokki had no official connection to either group, the Talons were available to follow his directives. His link was Dr. Xyntius, president of the Failure Club and supposed head of the Talons, who was also a physics professor in Michigan. Sokki had become the professor's confidante during a political campaign—third-party futility—and now supplied the planning for a more effective effort. Finding that the website had nothing new of interest, he opened his computer file on the Failure Club membership. To expand the sabotage of the Talons they would need to recruit more operatives, and the Failure Club was their ersatz talent pool.

While Sokki had a legitimate landscaping business, there

was no sign of it in the apartment. He left it entirely at his facility in a nearby commercial zone, thus maintaining total control of his personal environment. The business was another sort of cover, he thought, giving him an acceptable shell in Canadian society. He'd learned it while working for someone else, gaining an extensive knowledge of decorative stone and perennials. His reputation spread and he was offered a lucrative partnership in Montreal. He turned the latter down, to Alypia's chagrin. He'd also been invited to bid on a government contract in Ottawa, but he chose to stay in Windsor, on the edges of his two countries. He would sometimes have a job around Detroit, embellishing a condo development or an industrial park. With NAFTA and his dual citizenship, the border was his oyster.

Alypia arrived while he was at the computer. She took a seat beneath Modigliani's mistress while Sokki eased back in the recliner. He'd taken a Cuban cigar from the nearby humidor and proceeded to light up.

"Do you really enjoy those," Lyp asked, "or are you making a statement?"

"Enjoy? It's for the experience. I'm not a leftist. I'm a classicist."

"No, you're not."

"Well, except with you."

Lyp smiled, only a small change in her face. She had strong features, with deep-set eyes amid an olive complexion. Her brown hair was full and wavy. Two decades younger than Sokki, she was big-boned but had no excess weight.

"You look like an old robber baron," she said.

"A laissez faire? Wedded to the British banking houses? Bush's relatives?"

She laughed.

"That would make you a Bush."

Sokki looked away from her, toward the window.

"Old Prescott, playing both sides in World War II. Financed the arms buildup for Germany, among others. Then he fattened up as a Cold War senator, teaching George the ropes. Those same British banks financed George the First's campaigns. Always money and war, war and money—colonies along the way."

"And the CIA."

"Ah yes, protecting national security by making enemies around the world."

"All for freedom."

"Yeah, freedom—the freedom of the banking class via Big Oil and the war industries. Honored with songs before every ball game."

"Easy now, Sokki. You're on the good side of the border."

"He looked at her lazily with his long, thin smile, eyes half closed.

"You *make* it good," he said.

Lyp smiled again, but with a stir in her shoulders. So, Sokki thought, it's time for some business. He put out his cigar.

"I take it," he said, "there's news from the guild."

Lyp hesitated.

"Yes, they were impressed. The total destruction, everyone escaping—it was quite efficient for a new group."

"Why do I get the feeling this is a good and bad news thing?"

"Well, after all, Sokki, bombing a toilet facility along a highway! There's a question of significance. If they're going to help you, they want to feel it'll be worthwhile."

"Okay, I get the picture. Actually, it was an expensive rest area building with all major systems, a real problem to replace under a strained state budget. But why quibble? Of *course* we'll be going for bigger things! This gig was just to develop the group."

"Sort of a training run? An exercise?"

"Exactly."

She nodded, appraising now.

"So when does training day phase into hitting some high-priority targets?"

"Real soon, maybe next time out. We need to recruit a few more operatives, but we've got a tested, efficient core now. You yourself said they did well."

Lyp shrugged.

"It's a step up from burning the bus garage."

They shared a laugh.

"That was suggested by one of the Talons. An inner-city guy."

"They'll laugh about it themselves as they move on."

"I'm sure."

"Are you hungry yet? I didn't stop for lunch."

They decided to walk to Beau Jim's, a quiet restaurant on the way to the nightclub strip. The evening crowd was not yet gathering, so they got in easily without a reservation. Sokki ordered fillet of sole, which came lightly nestled on Boston lettuce, while Lyp had a petite filet mignon.

"You look envious," she said, having caught Sokki eyeing her steak.

"Ah, well. The demands of advancing age."

"You're not old. Anyway, we have the good health care. Not like over there."

She tilted her head toward the United States.

"Yeah," Sokki agreed. "They soak you on insurance premiums, but then you get wiped out anyway by medical bills."

"The doctors could stop it, if they wanted to."

"Well, the same doctors are on the boards of both hospitals and insurance companies. They decide both how much to charge and how much to cover. So they still take all they can from you *after* taking the alleged insurance."

"That's terrible."

"There's financial shams everywhere, with the government's blessing. Caveat emptor. Get up each morning at your own financial risk."

"It'll take some doing to put a dent in that system."
"Medical?"
"No, the whole corporate organism, with its government lackeys."
"Well, that's what we're about, Lyp."
"Uh-huh."
She chewed her steak with obvious relish.
"You know, Sokki, another thing came up in the guild. The 'no casualties' dictate that you give your operatives. I mean, insisting on property damage only is ultimately going to limit your effectiveness."

Sokki gave her his stare, disarming to most people. Lyp had long since adjusted to it, however.

"The basic appeal of our work," he said, "is that we take a higher moral ground than our adversary. That's how we recruit people. Why should they join if we ourselves seem morally questionable?"

"I understand, but I'm not talking about recruitment. I'm talking about down the road, as your projects progress. Maybe you should loosen the shackles a bit. After all, if the other side senses your limits, they could write you off as just some latter-day hippie, or guru. Purely symbolic, and no threat to them personally."

Sokki tried the smile.
"Well, we know that's not true."
"Yes, but *they* don't. That's the point."
"So then, we're talking bodily harm? That's the price for support from the guild?"
"Not harm in the gratuitous sense. You know I'd never support something like that. But when it comes to selected targets, individuals—well, they think you should be more flexible."

Flexible, Sokki thought—his own polemic being sprung against him. Lyp was learning, all right. Or maybe it was the guild—even better.

"Are you having dessert?" he asked.

"Of course!"

After they left Beau Jim's, they decided to take a walk through the nightclub strip. It was starting to gain momentum for Saturday night. Most of the people they saw were younger than Lyp, with all being younger than Sokki. They skirted the waiting lines, looked away from the brighter lights, ignored the pulsing music. When they came to a side street with a used-book store, Sokki suggested they turn off. The store was still open, though it would close within the hour.

"There's one like this in Montreal," Lyp said as they browsed. "I think of you when I'm in it."

Ah, Sokki thought, the token appeal. Once every visit, Lyp hinted he should move to Montreal.

"Well, there's the business," he preemptively explained, "and now—well, the other business stateside."

He glanced around, hinting that they should limit their discussion. Alypia understood.

"Ever think of going back? For good, I mean."

"What, stateside? You've got to be kidding."

"Well, with retirement coming up, not that far off—just thought I'd ask."

"I last considered it before Reagan. Then came trickle-down economics, the series of gratuitous wars and support for death squads, dictators. Stuff like 'ketchup is a vegetable'—remember that? To avoid spending more on school lunch programs?"

"Vaguely. I was busy with the separatists then."

"Yeah. Well, that put the kibosh on my American Dream. The more standard version, I mean."

"What would you call your current version?"

"Not so much a dream. More like a prophecy."

He gave her the smile. This time she returned it, nodding a bit against the bookstore background. Sokki suggested they leave.

"Of course," Lyp said outside, "there are plenty of

movements over there, in your other country."

"Useless, most of them. The corporate types just laugh at them, use the media to marginalize, defuse, shape public opinion against them."

"Not to mention using the government."

Sokki gazed into the far distance, his long strides forcing Lyp to step quickly to keep up.

"Tell you what, Lyp. Time's starting to run short for me. Movements as such don't have much meaning—I mean *promise,* for seeing results in my lifetime. Direct action, yes. Drastic moves to guarantee results. That's our business, right? So I'm willing, you know, to step things up like you and the guild say. I'm agreeable."

They'd stopped at a quiet corner. Small trees were planted in squares of earth amid the cement. Sokki's professional eye judged the workmanship. Alypia smoothed her hair in the chill wind that had risen.

"So *how* willing are you, Sokki? Can we say that the ban on casualties is off?"

"I have an idea," Sokki replied, "something that will tie in with my plan for multiple strikes in our next project. Two venues—one government target and one corporate, thus making transition to our main enemy. Well, I'll keep that much. But I'll drop the ban on casualties and even make fatalities our goal—only they won't be human."

Lyp continued to push her hair back in the wind, conditioned against surprise at anything Sokki might say.

"We'll go after animals they own. Expensive pets, prize livestock, and such. Time the two strikes so there's no doubt about their connection."

"The owners being two prominent figures."

"Right. Maybe cabinet level, CEO, CFO, COO—"

Alypia looked away, let her hair fly.

"It beats blowing up toilets," she said.

They walked back to Sokki's apartment by a route away

from the strip. The streets were dimly lit with few pedestrians, though car traffic was steady. Sokki was in his element, a phantom in the night, but he knew that Lyp wanted more. She was gregarious, found things dead in this city, or trite. Perhaps, without expressing it, she also felt that way about his operations. To reassure her, when they reached the apartment, he told of an idea to expand his shell organization, the Failure Club. To move beyond the Midwest, they might join with a group in the Atlanta area, ostensibly a reading club but given to radical existentialist philosophy. They would thus have an additional pool from which to recruit militants for the Talons of the Phoenix.

"This came from your front man, Dr. Xyntius?"

"No, it's my own research. Protected identity, of course."

"Actually, we know about them. All very young and/or intellectual. Not much potential as operatives. Maybe for a safe house in the area. Not much more."

Sokki's gaze dropped to the floor, swung to the partially smoked cigar at his side. He considered relighting it, smoking away this gap in the evening.

"There's another possibility," said Lyp, "much better in our view."

"Oh?"

"It involves the Earth Freedom Force."

"Destroyers of rustic condos and gas-hog vehicles?"

"Well, this is a rogue cell, or cluster. More chutzpah than the EFF in general. They've been known to harass, intimidate, even one brief kidnapping. Someone in the guild has contact with them."

"Where do they operate?"

"Alberta and B.C. on our side, and the states southward down to Salt Lake, where your guy can meet with them."

"They cover a big area."

"But not much population. They're looking to expand their impact, sort of like you. Get beyond the regional and explode some issues nationally. They won't insist on staying with the environment."

Sokki lit his partial cigar, savored this offer of new power, unexpected progress.

"Do you have someone you can send to Salt Lake?" Lyp asked. "Clean, and low visibility?"

"Uh-huh, this young guy we just moved up. Has a master's and he's a marksman, too. Learned it hunting, no military. His name is Andrew."

"So shall I set it up?"

"Yeah, go ahead."

"Okay. And you're welcome."

Sokki smiled as he started to puff.

"I don't ever take you for granted, Lyp."

She eyed him through the smoke. Business, Sokki thought, is close to finishing for the day.

"I've got plenty of wine," he said. "Like a booster?"

"That would be nice."

They sipped the red wine without saying much, holding up their glasses to view the color. Lyp smiled coyly after a while, but it wasn't yet the bedroom look. She was still holding back.

"Can you use a SAM?" she asked.

"A *what*?"

"Surface-to-air missile."

Sokki started to smile, but of course she wasn't kidding. This wasn't just Alypia speaking; it was the guild.

"Getting a bit ahead of ourselves, aren't we?"

"If you want to score big, you'll need the right equipment. We could slip it into a machinery shipment, or you could take it over with your own junk."

"Junk? Oh, you mean the noble tools of my profession."

Lyp was silent. Maybe it wasn't really crazy, he thought, just seemed that way to his staid methodology. While flexible, he'd been prone to strong caution.

"Can they afford to give one up? Surely a SAM was on their own wish lists."

"Well, there's something heavier on the way." She hesitated, then "A mini-nuke."

"Come on."

"They got access to a prototype from a British research intern. The hot stuff they pick up in Ukraine."

"Still for the highest bidder, hey?"

"Actually, it's rather cheap now."

Sokki swirled wine in his glass, letting the news sink in. Perhaps he'd been moving too slowly.

"I'll take the SAM," he said. "And thank you, Lyp."

She smiled without replying. Her work is done, Sokki thought, so she can relax. But was not her work also his? This help they were giving him, as they gave it to others, was part of an effort to establish a wide pattern of actions. The eventual effect of these mounting actions would be to force change—perhaps collapse—of the overriding order that gripped the planet. As the Soviet Union had fallen, and the colonial empires before them, so would corporate hegemony. His goal and Lyp's in this effort were the same, so since her work was done for the day so was his. They could relax as they worked—together.

As was their custom, he let her prepare in the bedroom while he finished his day in the computer room. Standing before the full-wall montage, his chronicle of corruption in the world's master nation, Sokki felt empowered to move decisively against it. Had the offers of help been made by anyone but Lyp, he'd have been skeptical, even cynical. But she was the only person with whom he was intimate, and her commitment against the enemy was pure, so this new sense of strength was genuine. If he had to relax his self-imposed limits, so be it. It wasn't as if he were stooping to his adversaries' level. They were a world problem, exploiting its peoples and resources. He was the antidote.

Glancing sideways at the world map, he considered the pervasiveness of international finance and its intrigues. U.S. corporations were themselves, in a sense, agents of this international force, though also the largest part of it. On both levels there were increasing mergers and other concentrations of power, simplifying the lobbying efforts and other controls on the U.S. government. Through this government, and perhaps Israel's, the financiers could use the American military as their world police force. The Atlanticists in Britain, of course, were willing to add their soldiers, too, to profit their big banking houses. Opposition to this process, however mundane, could get you tagged as "the enemy," while the military was glorified more than ever. They were fighting, after all, for the success of the corporate dream—unlimited plunder of the earth and its inhabitants.

Turning to the wall behind him, Sokki studied the forty or so mug shots that were taped to the wall in a triangular arrangement. Fairly high in the display was the controlling heir to a chemical company, one that had made napalm for the Vietnam War. The bland, fuzzy image attracted Sokki now because he recalled that the man owned race horses. His company had lately gained higher emissions limits from the EPA, represented in the photos by a female face near the bottom. This moved Sokki to consult the Internet for data on the EPA official. Sure enough, there she was with a pair of prize Afghan hounds, their coats lovingly brushed. So, thought Sokki, all we need to do is rate the chemical man's horses, figure the top one, and we have our targets for the Talons. Two venues, simultaneous strikes. The corporate-political link will be unmistakable, as will our message.

"Are you coming to bed soon?" Lyp asked.

She was standing in the doorway, wearing a midnight-blue nightgown he'd given her.

"Right now," Sokki answered. "I'll just log off."

She lingered as he finished and put out the light. He draped a long arm over her shoulders as they moved into the glow from the bedroom. He could have done more tonight, he knew, but he wouldn't let warfare come between him and Lyp. The barbarians had disrupted his life, but they would not prevent his ecstasy.

CHAPTER 5

On a chill November morning, two men with M16s lay in a park in upscale Maryland. Their colleague pretended to walk casually on an adjacent street, near their van. They were from the Talons of the Phoenix, a group of social militants who were striking at two venues this morning. The attacks would be simultaneous. The false stroller, known as Bar, would coordinate with the other venue via cell phone. He checked a number now through rimless glasses, pressed *send*, and nudged the phone into shaggy dark-blond hair. A phone rang at the other venue, a horse farm in Virginia, and was answered by Mary Ellen, a female Talon.

"What's your status?" Bar asked.

"Subject finished his morning run, browsing in field. Messenger in position."

"Time window?"

"Twenty minutes or so. Your status?"

"Expect visual within five minutes, messengers in positions."

"Will stand by. Disconnect?"

"Disconnect."

The two men with M16s were The Private, a stocky senior member of the Talons, and Collins, who was tall and sometimes giddy. Mindful of the other venue, he'd twice started humming "In the Blue Ridge Mountains of Virginny." The Private immediately silenced him, quashing a potential warning to the targets, which were now coming into view along with their handler. They were two Afghan hounds of high pedigree, the property of an executive who regulated the environment. Bar, the gunmen's cohort, now made another call to Virginia, where a prize race horse belonging to a chemical heir was about to be executed. The heir's company had recently been relieved of emissions restrictions by the environmental official.

"Subjects approaching operation site," said Bar.

"Now alerting messenger," Mary Ellen replied.

Bar realized she was signaling Andrew, the gunman at her venue, who was using a large-caliber hunting rifle.

"Sporadic progress into open area," Bar continued. "Delivery imminent, within the minute."

"Our messenger ready. Locked onto subject."

Reaching the center of a wide grassy area, the handler unhooked the leads from the dogs' collars, as was his habit. The well-trained dogs didn't run, but pranced about freely within easy calling range. The handler brought out his cigarettes and lit up. Concealed in vegetation and shadows, The Private and Collins leveled their M16s. Bar was returning to the van, preparing to slide into the driver's seat. He glanced back at the long-haired dogs, their brushed coats shimmering even though it was overcast.

Muffled gunshots pierced the gray morning. The dog farthest from the handler flew back like a rag and lay still. The other dog rolled and lay struggling to get up. Two more shots put an end to its struggle.

"Delivery made," said Bar. "Departing venue and will disconnect."

"Notifying messenger. Disconnect."

Bar heard a snap on the other end just before the connection was broken. One horse down, he thought. The Private and Collins hustled into the van, their weapons concealed in garbage bags. The parcels would be flung into a local river a short distance away. Bar drove off at a moderate speed, careful to observe all traffic laws.

"How's the handler doing?" he asked.

"Froze on the first volley," said The Private. "Hit the ground on the second, face down. Didn't see shit."

Collins had his mouth open but was quiet, looking sheepish. Bar assumed it was his miss that had led to the second volley. He wouldn't ask, though. They had to focus on their escape until they were clear.

"Hook up with Virginia okay?" The Private asked.

"No problem. Think I heard the shot even."

"Good. Everything following specs, then. Good."

"Think we both hit our second shots?" Collins asked.

"Hey, it don't matter. All that matters is we covered it. Ain't no merit badges on this."

Collins stared out a window, not satisfied. When they reached the river, Bar pulled off the road and The Private told Collins to pitch the bags. As he carried out the task, Collins disappeared behind some trees on the embankment.

"I don't know about this guy," The Private remarked. "He's been shaky right along."

Bar shrugged.

"Looks like we'll get through the day okay."

"Yeah, but we're gonna have heavier stuff down the pike. I maybe should talk to Lyme about it."

Bar pictured Dr. Lyme, secretary of the Failure Club, their shell organization from which Talons were recruited. The Club, ostensibly, was still just a social group for losers that advertised on the Internet.

"Lyme would know what to do," Bar agreed. "Think we should wipe the plates yet?"

They had dirtied the van's license plates to foil possible witnesses.

"Nah, we're still too close. We'll get'em when we stop for lunch. With the guns gone, it don't matter if we're stopped for it."

They heard a distinct splash through The Private's lowered window. An identical second splash followed.

"Christ," muttered The Private, "hope there ain't no joggers out."

"No, too crappy a day."

"Hope you're right."

Collins returned and Bar pulled away smoothly. He'd drive directly to the interstate, then start back to the Midwest. The Talons had been a regional force up to now, but today's actions would establish them nationally. Bar felt good as he drove, sensing he was part of something great. He could never do much as an individual, being isolated by the system into mediocrity. Thanks to the Talons, he was born again in a non-religious way, living a new life of war for reform. He felt eager for what lay ahead.

"So," he said, "you say there's heavier stuff down the pike?"

"Yeah," The Private answered, then glanced back at Collins. "But maybe we oughta just think about lunch for now. Know what I mean?"

"Right," Bar answered.

He drove on beneath the heavy gray sky.

• • •

Andrew's shot was perfect, so his father would have been proud if the victim weren't a horse. On many a chill morning they'd trudged the Wisconsin woods together, hoping to put down a deer with the skill he'd just shown. But his father's eyesight was poor and Andrew lacked motivation, killing for sport being a secret issue for him. Working with the Talons, however, his motivation was strong and pure. Be it horse or deer or elephant, he'd gladly shoot an animal if it loosened the corporate stranglehold. For other reasons, yes, killing was wrong. But he wanted a progressive society for his baby daughter and her generation, and that meant reversing the social neglect and cultural decay fostered by financiers and their stooges in government. The horse today was an innocent victim, but its demise was necessary for the Talons' cause.

While he was in charge of this venue today, Andrew was the youngest in his crew. He was trimly built with light brown hair and handsome features. He contrasted with Mary Ellen, his liaison to the other venue, who was stocky with salt-and-pepper hair. She was a nurse who'd served in international relief efforts, including the Balkans, Africa, and the Middle East. She'd joined the Talons through her paramour, The Private, and until recently had been the only female member. Their driver for the day was Sludge, a new recruit from the Failure Club. His real name was Dave, but members of the Failure Club, and hence the Talons, went by the handle of their choosing. Sludge was tall but tended to slouch. He would have been strong if he weren't out of shape, but he still had a menacing look due to his overhanging brows. He was a former federal bureaucrat who now worked as a mechanic.

"That was a nice gun you ditched," Sludge remarked. "Too bad you couldn't save the scope, at least. Nicest I've seen."

"We always stick strictly to plan," said Andrew from the back. "That way we stay undetected."

As at the Maryland venue, the weapon of execution had been dropped in a river, though Andrew had broken it down first. He'd stood on the overgrown bank and created five splashes as if he were throwing stones. But the "stones" were the rifle's three parts, the high-quality scope, and the suppressor, or silencer. There was a ceremonial quality to the disposal and Andrew wanted to linger, but the plan said to drive at once to Richmond, to the airport. They'd turn in the rental car from Indiana and escape Virginia by air.

"We stopping for lunch?" asked Sludge.

"Yes," Andrew replied, "but a fast-food place. Less chance

of being ID'd. And park away from the building." Then, to Mary Ellen, "You're awfully quiet. The other venue?"

"Uh-huh. I can't help it."

"You were in touch, though. Everything went okay, didn't it?"

"Yeah, up to when they broke off—right after their action. Too bad we can't check."

"Right. But we don't know what the lackeys are using to monitor calls. Whatever it is, it clicks in as soon as they link the actions, maybe before."

"So we can't know how they are. And they're driving back. A long ways."

"How come they're not flying?" asked Sludge.

"In case the lackeys cross-check passenger lists," said Andrew. "So they don't catch similarities between the Maryland crew and us."

"That's good," Mary Ellen acknowledged. "Our leaders know what they're doing."

Andrew admired her dedication, knowing that she and The Private were intimate. Still, he sensed a problem in couples working on projects together. He himself would never have to deal with it, since his wife was oblivious to his work for the Talons. As far as she knew, he was away on some quixotic political quest for the Failure Club. It was better that way, he thought. Not everyone was suited to fighting corporate vermin and their lackeys. Mary Ellen was exceptional, even as she sat in front of him watching the South roll by.

"By the way," he said to her, "I hear they have a one-woman project waiting for you."

"Okkura, you mean? That's sort of a mentoring thing. Whatever, I don't mind. With another female Talon, I don't have to be one of the guys all the time."

"Aw, what's wrong with that?" Sludge kidded.

"Nothing," she said simply, and looked back to the scenery.

"You and I have something, too, Sludge," Andrew continued. "That is, if you're agreeable."

"Shooting more horses?"

"No, nothing like today. Actually, it's just a sort of meeting, hanging out. But it's out west, with people we don't know. Dr. Xyntius wants to make an alliance with a group out there."

Dr. Xyntius, president of the Failure Club and head of the Talons, informed them of necessary projects and long-range planning. The secretary of the club, Dr. Lyme, was the only other officer knowledgeable of the Talons. They were under his supervision while in action on projects.

"Hey," said Sludge, "any way I can help. I'll work it out with the shop. They know they owe me. Not like those assholes before."

"The Feds?"

"Yeah. Pea-brains. I wouldn't wish them on anyone. You should see the managers. Strutting around, proud of their GS levels—pay grades, basically. Then they get a memo from upstairs and it's like a live wire in their genitals!"

He looked over at Mary Ellen, who didn't react, then back to the road.

"Anyway, the unit stands in a circle when someone gets an award or promotion, forty-some people in an office of 2,700. One of the managers reads a manifesto praising the person, ending dramatically with—*ta-da!*—the name! The people standing around all start clapping—on cue, it's expected—with the bigger brownnoses cheering and shouting comments. Then the honoree has to thank the lackey manager. It's enough to make you puke!"

"Yeah, well, now you're out of there, Sludge. And you're working *against* that phoniness—the endless charades that support corporate power."

"And we're working with you," Mary Ellen added.

"Our loyalty to each other is genuine," Andrew continued, "and absolute. There's no phoniness in the Talons."

Sludge nodded solemnly, at the same time watching for a restaurant.

JAMES I. MCGOVERN

• • •

    The day's last patient was gone from the Lyme Clinic of Chiropractic, as well as the doctor's regular assistant, so only Dr. Lyme and Okkura, a trainee, remained. While she was, in fact, learning to be a chiropractic assistant, Okkura was also in training for a more controversial role. She was a newly recruited member of the Talons of the Phoenix, the cadre of social militants that had struck at two venues this day. While she knew little of their operations, Okkura was happy to be with the Talons, and with Dr. Lyme, as an escape from her previous situation. A masseuse in an Indiana town, she'd faced mounting prostitution charges and would have done time were it not for Dr. Lyme's intervention. With tenacity and skill, he'd convinced her probation officer to recommend this placement for her rehabilitation.
    Though the office door was locked, Okkura continued to sit at the reception desk in her white uniform. She was without a car and a stranger to this area, the northern Chicago suburbs, so Dr. Lyme would take her to her apartment. Okkura had reddish-blond hair tied back for the office, clear brown eyes, and a pert nose. She looked good in the office and gave it charm, but she wasn't at all needed for the practice. Her value lay entirely in her being a second female Talon, thus expanding the possibilities for their actions. Her skill as a masseuse and her erotic sideline added deception to the Talons' arsenal. Bringing her in was a key accomplishment for Dr. Lyme, highly satisfying and appreciated, no doubt, by those higher up.
    The chiropractor washed up now after a hectic day, having shed his "doc smock." He'd eventually heard from The Private and Andrew, calling after gaining 100 miles on their respective venues. To all appearances the Talons had swept a doubleheader. He'd forwarded the results to Dr. Xyntius, using cryptic language for security. They'd speak more freely later, away from the ears of students and patients. Dr. Lyme smiled as he thought of the day's patients, the extra gusto with

which he'd snapped their spines around. Oh well, he thought, spread the wealth. Give them some benefit from the Talons' victories. Actually, of course, it had been a release of tension for him. The stress of supervising the attacks was itself difficult, but he'd also been unable to discuss it with anyone. Okkura was a newbie, only vaguely aware of the project.

"You look tired," she said when he came out.

"Now, why would that be, I wonder?"

He was still holding a towel, dabbing at stray drops around his ears. His sandy hair, normally a smooth, styled mane, was tousled now. The goatee he wore was damp.

"I could give you a massage."

"Mm, sounds good. I was just trying to figure how to give myself an adjustment."

"No, seriously. It's a great way to unwind."

"Well, I guess I need *something*. It was a great day for the Talons, but fitting it in with the practice was a bitch. Beg your parsnips."

"You should have taken off, maybe."

"Nope. Alibis make us undetectable, and that's where our strength lies. Mary Ellen will cover all that with you."

Okkura nodded, appearing thoughtful.

"You okay?" Lyme asked. "Today and all, I mean?"

She brightened, returning to the room and the man.

"Sure. Will it be on the news, do you think?"

"I heard a snippet on the radio before. Just the horse. Don't worry. They'll put two plus one together by tomorrow. Takes them awhile. That's why they work for the government."

He gave her a wink. Okkura smiled in well-conditioned response.

"So," she said, "how about that massage?"

He hesitated. Then, "Why not?"

Dr. Lyme was normally cautious in his personal involvements. He was married, after all, with two school-age children. He had a spacious suburban home and an established practice. As secretary of the Failure Club, he was top aide to the president, Dr. Xyntius, since the vice president was a senile figurehead (or figureneck, as Dr. Lyme would say). Within that shell group, of course, he was a key figure in the Talons—the hub of operations, in fact. This was his role that most needed protection, which could not be compromised. With Okkura, however, that role was already known, so he saw no danger in consenting to a massage. Fully mindful of what it might lead to, he led her to one of the treatment rooms and a padded table on which he adjusted spines.

"Do you have some kind of oil?" she asked.

"Just conductant for the stimulator."

The machine stood near the table, with pads attached by wires for shooting voltage into bodies.

"It'll do, I guess."

Dr. Lyme stripped to his shorts. Mounting the table, he wasn't surprised to see that Okkura had slipped out of her uniform.

"I can work better this way," she said.

I'm sure you can, he thought.

After just briefly rubbing with conductant, her hands left his back. He saw her bra join her uniform over a nearby chair. The rubbing continued.

"Feels good."

"I'll just loosen you up a bit, get rid of the strain. Relax with me, now."

"Yes, mother."

She slapped him on the shorts. Soon after, she was sliding them off while he accommodated her. The shorts and her panties were filed on the chair. He felt her mounting the table above him—her knees bumping his thighs, her breasts grazing his back. She continued the rubbing, but with a full-body motion now, grinding herself into him.

"Time to flip over," he said after a while.

She was ready to stay on top, but he laid her down on the table.

"Around here," he said, "this is the view I'm used to."

Using a condom, he probed her slowly, reflectively. There was nothing wrong with this, he thought. It was a bonding between Talons, as well as Okkura's favor to him, her benefactor. And he deserved this, he had it coming. He was working to level the playing field against the corporate types, including the M.D.'s and their insurance allies. Call him a quack, would they? Second or third-rate? Well, how many of *them* got to have action like *this*?

He accelerated his thrusts. The mingled moans of man and woman floated through the medical suite, perhaps distracting a mouse or two.

• • •

The large, well-dressed bald man attracted little attention as he waited in the fancy hotel lobby. The hotel, after all, rose among hives of corporate ambition. But the business of Dr. Xyntius was not financial profit. He was there as head of the Talons of the Phoenix, responsible for recent political killings of prize animals. He'd taken a short flight from Michigan to meet with Dr. Lyme, his lieutenant in the Talons, regarding their immediate plans. Dr. Xyntius would have driven, but there were ample funds for flying now thanks to the Talons' friends in Canada. The infusion of funds was technically into the Failure Club, their shell organization, and might prove an accounting challenge to Mr. Singh, the club's treasurer. But, since he was oblivious to the Talons' existence, Mr. Singh was a convenient buffer against outside suspicion. Any problems with their finances could be blamed on his incompetence.

Dr. Lyme arrived in the lobby, striding aggressively through the maze of couches. He was wearing beige-rimmed glasses to match his hair and goatee, mildly irritating Dr. Xyntius. Besides having conservative tastes, the professor saw no point in making themselves more noticeable.

"Feel like Italian today?" Lyme inquired, referring to their impending lunch.

"I've the appetite for it," Xyntius replied. "Just so we can hear each other."

"But no one else can, right? I know just the place."

There was a huge shopping mall near the hotel, but they drove past it to a restaurant next to a business park.

"Well," Lyme said on the way, "guess we're finally hitting our stride."

"Yes, the teams did well. So did you, Allan. I'm sure they were pleased up north."

"We earned our wings, so to speak?"

"They're increasing support, yes. I'll elaborate over lunch. Success goes better with food."

He wanted to parcel things out to Lyme, make sure he understood. Greater activity called for more attention to control. Success opened doors to them, but not every task would be pleasant. Changes might have to be made, weaknesses dealt with. He wasn't sure that Lyme, with his flamboyant style, was up to such subtleties.

"How's it going with Okkura?" he asked over his meal.

"Great. She's bonding with Mary Ellen this week. I excused her from the practice."

"Fine. She could be very useful for us. Valuable, in fact. I admire your management of her."

Dr. Lyme glanced up from his pasta but didn't speak. He nodded away the compliment.

"Of course," Dr. Xyntius continued, "our other new one, Sludge, has already been on a project. We should get Okkura some action, too."

"The trip to Salt Lake?"

"No, on that I see Derek and Sludge going with Andrew. Protection, if you will. A nice compact group with just one talker. We want smart, simple negotiations with this Earth Freedom Force."

"Rogue cell, right?"

"Two, actually. Made their own little alliance. It's

something Andrew should be aware of, that he's dealing with two more or less equal leaders."

Xyntius hesitated, put down his fork.

"You should know, Allan, I'll be talking directly with Andrew, one-on-one, before he goes. It's no reflection on you. I just want to be perfectly clear with him on some details. The fewer links in communication between myself and the EFF, the better I'll feel."

Dr. Lyme stopped eating.

"Well, I could be present, anyway."

"I'm thinking that—just this once—I'll be the field supervisor. You'll know what's going on, don't worry. And Andrew will understand that this doesn't diminish your role with us."

Momentarily perplexed, Lyme relaxed into an affable smile.

"Guess you *do* speak his language better. He's a very bright guy. No problem, Jon."

He dug back into his pasta. He was clever, Xyntius thought, however careless he was. His value to them was still great, therefore, as was the threat he posed if alienated.

"I appreciate your understanding, Allan. Actually, though, there's another reason I'm relieving you a bit. We have another action of a sort that you'll have to keep an eye on: a sensitive shipment to the Failure Club at its regular meeting place, the Galactic Retreat Center. A team of Talons will have to retrieve it—discreetly—from our landlords, the monks."

"A shipment? Yes, the gurus sign but don't open anything. Some cover there. But why the high-pressure pickup?"

"There are two SAMs inside."

Dr. Lyme bent close.

"Surface-to-air missiles?"

"Yes."

"Holy shit! You mean, just sitting there in boxes, two neat packages with bar codes on them?"

"Not exactly. They're mixed in with some old bottling

equipment from Canada, supposedly for a Failure Club project."

"A disclaimer, right? Someone else stuck them in?"

"If necessary. But it shouldn't *be* necessary. We'll want a nice, clean pickup and transport to The Private's cache in Ohio."

Lyme had kept his head low, intensely interested. He'd apparently forgotten about Andrew and Salt Lake, which pleased Dr. Xyntius. Now the chiropractor looked away, reflecting.

"Well, we could keep the dog detail together, since they're going to The Private's place anyway. Of course, there's the thing about Collins."

"Yes," said Xyntius, "which is why he shouldn't go. At the same time, it's a chance to involve Okkura. She can just ride along, basically. The Private and Bar can handle the work."

Dr. Lyme frowned.

"Right. But what do we tell Collins? Putting him on the shelf—I mean, he's been active right along."

"Tell him whatever you need to, Allan. We're entering new territory now, with people behind us and beside us who are ready to go farther, to be more radical then we'd planned."

"The SAMs."

"Yes, and all that they imply. It's a test for us, our commitment to our basic goal. If some of our cherished values get in the way, we have to be willing to set them aside, and set aside *people* who aren't working out."

Sitting straight now, Dr. Lyme nodded.

"Whatever you say, Jon. We'll do what it takes."

Dr. Xyntius reached for the wine bottle and filled their glasses.

• • •

Bar slowed the van as they approached the familiar driveway, the long stretch of gravel leading to the Galactic Retreat Center. The Private rode next to him with Okkura in back, along with a litter of rugs and computer boxes. The two SAMs they were picking up would be hidden within the litter. The Talons would move on immediately, to all eyes just a van full of people and junk. They'd roll through Indiana to Ohio with their contraband undetected.

Though Okkura was new, Bar was more comfortable with her than with Collins. Okkura was alert, eager to help, and didn't cause problems. Collins had seemed to drift in his own world and even The Private had trouble working with him. With the long drives, the stops to eat and sleep, and the projects themselves, it was important that they work with someone who was steady, who wouldn't compromise them. They gave up some expertise in Collins, but today it wasn't needed anyway. Okkura's presence made it easier on the road and at stops, and Bar guessed it wouldn't hurt during the pickup.

They pulled up to the large, barn-like structure, nestled in the woods with a field for parking and camping. The building's white paint and green shingles looked thin and weathered in the December sunlight. Three large wooden crates stood near one of the entrances.

"They're right out in the open," Bar remarked.

"It's okay," said The Private. "They just came this morning. If it was gonna rain, we woulda called the gurus to put a tarp on."

"So who's in charge here?"

"Head guru's named Sho. Prob'ly hanging with one or two flunkies. Won't be no problem."

They parked the van and got out to examine the crates, Okkura bringing up the rear.

"How can we take all that in the van?" she asked.

"We ain't," The Private answered. "We'll pick and choose."

He looked over one of the crates.

"Shit. We got some heavy-duty woodwork here. Tell you what, look for good places to pry while I get the tire iron."

He returned to the van. Bar became aware of a short young man standing in the nearby doorway. He had a cherubic face, dark hair parted in the middle, and he wore a windbreaker above baggy pants.

"Hi," said Bar. "Are you Sho?"

"Superior Sho went to town. I am Mohar."

"We're from the Failure Club. We came to pick up the shipment."

The monk looked at him blankly, then shifted his gaze to Okkura.

"I'm Okkura," she offered. "This is Bar. That's, um, The Private."

Mohar appeared confused.

"Do you have identification? From the club?"

Bar's membership card was on his bureau half a state away. He didn't want the words "Failure Club" in his wallet. He doubted that The Private had a card, either. Fortunately, Okkura was digging in her purse as if she carried hers. It soon emerged from a tangle of items and was received by Mohar with great reverence.

"What's goin' on?" asked The Private, walking up with a tire iron and a claw hammer.

"We had to show credentials," Bar explained.

"Fuck that shit. C'mon, we got work to do."

He handed Bar the claw hammer. They set to work prying at the crates while Okkura and the monk looked on. No one else appeared. The Private got his crate open first and motioned to Bar to have a look inside.

"There's one of the stingers with the bottling junk crammed against it. I see a grip-stock near the bottom. So one more of each, then two apiece of the scopes and the cooling units."

"Got it."

The Private glanced at the two spectators.

"Why's he hanging around? We gotta fish these out to the van, unobserved."

"Let's find the other pieces," Bar suggested. "Maybe he'll leave in the meantime."

"Right."

They attacked the second and third crates while Okkura managed some conversation with Mohar. Unfortunately, the monk stayed rooted to his spot, apparently enjoying their company, especially Okkura's. When all parts of the SAMs had been located, The Private leaned close to Bar as they peered into a box.

"That fucking guru is still mooning at us. We need to get this shit outta here."

"What, you think we'll have to clobber him?"

"I feel like it, but that'd blow our setup here." A hesitation, then "Go tell Okkura to get Moonface inside and give him some sugar."

"But he's a monk."

"Fuck it! Get going."

Bar sidled away, unsure how to phrase the order to Okkura. He also wondered if he were being a pimp. But he had no time. Leaning toward her on the side away from Mohar, he muttered into her ear.

"Private says take him inside and make love."

A laugh reflex played at the corners of Okkura's mouth, quickly controlled by the knowledge that she was a Talon, that The Private wasn't joking. Bar saw this as he moved on, heard her start coaxing almost at once.

"Mohar, listen. There's something I need you to help me with. You see—"

Glancing back out of earshot, Bar saw the monk listening earnestly, not at all embarrassed. He seemed to feel empowered while Okkura appeared meek. Together, they turned and went in the building.

"Did you see that?" Bar asked in surprise.

"We got lucky," The Private answered. "Let's jump on it now, move those stingers."

They eased the two long cylinders out of their

respective crates and carried them to the van, where they were secreted among the rugs. The other SAM components were slipped into empty computer boxes and placed under real computer equipment. The three crates of bottling junk were nailed shut as they'd been before. As the work was finished, The Private looked around in satisfaction.

"Nobody saw nothin'. All according to specs."

"You want me to get Okkura?" Bar asked.

"No, I'll do it. I gotta tell Moonface we're leaving the crates, give'm some bullshit. You get the van started, be ready to pull right out."

Back in the van, Bar started the motor and pulled a little closer to the doorway. Okkura and The Private came out with Mohar trailing, the monk looking confused again. Okkura was suppressing a smile while The Private was brisk and brusque. With the Talons aboard, Bar gunned the motor and left Mohar in flying dust.

"Have a good one!" shouted The Private with a wave.

When they'd rounded a curve in the driveway, Okkura exploded in laughter.

"They was holding hands," The Private explained, "chanting some kind of mantra."

"Having a hot old time, eh?"

"Great seduction there, Okkura. Hope he didn't wear you out."

"Aw, he's a sweet little guy. Just wanted to help with my spiritual needs. My oneness."

The Private laughed himself.

"Oneness, huh? Well, I'll spring for drinks to repair any damage he done. Good job, lady."

Bar pulled onto the blacktop and accelerated. He appreciated the mirth, the feelings of success, but as driver his work wasn't done. The dismantled SAMs felt like meteors behind him, hurtling toward unknown targets with his assistance. He hoped he was equal to this stepped-up militance. The Talons were his life now, so he had to do his part for them. He'd help the Talons hit their targets, and he'd try to enjoy it with them. He wanted to belong in every way.

CHAPTER 6

The van containing four men and a surface-to-air missile had proceeded smoothly from Ohio to Connecticut. It was somewhat cramped in the back, since the SAM components were concealed among rugs and computer boxes, but the driver and front passenger were entirely comfortable. The men were members of the Talons for Earth Freedom, an alliance of social militant groups. Until recently, the occupants of the van had been the Talons of the Phoenix, but their leadership had forged an alliance with a rogue cluster within the Earth Freedom Force, which was environmental in focus. The new organization would continue to oppose corporate control of society and government, as the Phoenix group had done, but with a global perspective and statements of responsibility for their actions.

Throughout the current trip, the van's front passenger seat had been occupied by Dr. Lyme. He was dressed in "office casual," his sandy hair and goatee fresh from the styling shop. He usually wore glasses, but was using contacts for this trip, wanting full use of his peripheral vision. He'd normally supervise an attack from afar, but for this one he'd be on-site.

BEYOND THE FAILURE CLUB

It was their first project under the new name and they were using equipment from backers in Canada. Extra effort was needed to retain the confidence of the other groups. If all went well, the Talons for Earth Freedom would surge in stature and have no trouble gaining support, both in dollars and in personnel.

The driving had been shared by Bar, the newest member on the trip, and Andrew, who had risen within the Talons and represented the Phoenix group at the alliance meeting. Andrew was actually the youngest in the van, his light brown hair cut clean, while Bar was shaggy with touches of gray. The fourth member of the team, The Private, was in back with the missile for the duration of the trip. He gazed out from his tousled dark curls and tinted glasses. While sometimes prone to anxiety, he'd shown a calm, purposeful demeanor during this trip. He'd be the one shouldering the SAM when launch time came.

"Of course," Dr. Lyme was saying, "it isn't the *concept* of incorporation we oppose. We don't want people to get *that* idea. In theory, the corporation is a neutral thing, established and accepted for two or three centuries. Nobody's looking to turn all businesses into mom-and-pop stores, including us."

"Then there's the non-business corporations," said Andrew.

"Right. Charities, schools, cities and towns. If we talk about dismantling *everything,* we become ideological wackos."

"Communists, maybe," said The Private.

"More like nihilists," Lyme continued. "They'd have nothing positive to link us with. We'd be seen as backward—social Luddites, Druids—the direct opposite of what we are: progressive."

"So," said Bar behind the wheel, "we want people to know it's just *certain* corporations we oppose."

He glanced at Lyme for confirmation.

"The *abuse* of incorporation, yes. Its use to consolidate power for nefarious purposes. Both specific instances and repeated patterns."

"With an eye, maybe," said Andrew, "toward world

corporate hegemony."

Dr. Lyme turned in his seat and smiled.

"You're getting ahead of me, son. But yeah, there's the big picture. The multinationals, their control of governments, whole regions of the world, war and peace."

"The wars," said The Private. "They show themselves in the wars."

"They try not to. But yes, they're usually there."

"So how do we get the word out, let people know we ain't wackos, just fighting these takeover assholes?"

"Well," said Lyme, "to an extent our actions speak for themselves. But I guess we're about to supplement those messages. Right, Andrew?"

He and The Private eyed their comrade expectantly.

"Yes," he answered, "it came out of the alliance. We're going to claim responsibility for our actions. That is, the TEF will. Our friends out west will do the claiming on this one."

"No shit," said The Private. "They claim the credit after *we* do the work?"

"The point is," said Dr. Lyme, "they *are* us. We're all one group, so they're taking credit for us, too."

"So what they gonna do? Make calls, send letters to editors?"

"Maybe," Andrew replied, "but for sure they'll spread it around the Internet. That's their specialty. The group they broke from was doing it right along."

"Can't a claim like that be traced?" asked Bar.

"Not the way they do it. Any investigation just leads to a dead end, a raid on an empty room."

"I can respect that," said Dr. Lyme. "And we'll be pooling our resources with them, data bases and such. Actually, they helped with the specs for this job we're on."

He looked out the window when no one answered. The reality of the western group's involvement had settled into the van, become a presence as they rode along. But there was also the reality of the project itself, growing more and more vivid as they neared their destination. Having met with the western group, Andrew was more adjusted to them than the others, so he dwelt more on the nature of the job ahead. It was a watershed for the Talons, since none of their previous actions had claimed a human life. But for Andrew it was something more, a personal crisis. His growing role within the Talons, as a leader and perhaps a planner, was conflicting with an old commitment to respect life in all its forms. He wanted to achieve the Talons' aims, to save future societies from corporate domination and abuse, but he didn't want to kill. In the end, he knew, he would do what was necessary. But he also knew that his private conflict would remain, raging in the next chamber of his psyche.

The target of the operation was Dick Hanlon, a news spinner who blathered for an hour each night in prime time. He set the tone for other shows on the network's stations, defending authoritarian government and the corporate agenda behind it. Any challenge to the power structure, its culture of nationalism and religiosity, he reviled. It wouldn't have been bad if he'd simply expressed his views; they were expressed by many others, anyway. But he insisted, echoing the claim of the network, that his treatment of the news was fair and balanced. To support this claim, he'd sometimes host the holder of an opposing view, whom he would then interrupt and shout down at will. It was this tendency to manipulate the news, by Hanlon and others at the propaganda network, that had to be taught a graphic lesson.

"Turnoff for Newbridge is coming up," said The Private.

"Got it," Bar acknowledged.

"We'll be at a local-brand motel," said Dr. Lyme. "No budget-chain place was close enough. If they get conversational, we're computer techies doing an installation."

"I don't like it," said The Private. "Too familiar."

"No, we're cool," said Lyme. "Loads of outsiders come through here, both business and pleasure. There's the nature reserves, historical sites, shit like that."

The Private grunted.

"So when do we case for the strike?"

"Tomorrow morning, very early. We have to drive a ways. We'll hang on the point and watch his copter pass. It'd be better if we didn't show the SAM yet."

"That's okay. I know how to handle it."

"We'll do just one run-through?" asked Andrew.

"One is plenty," said Lyme. "He's very precise in his schedule, obsessive-compulsive. We have our police and coast guard info, so we mostly just want to get a feel for the place."

"The cover," The Private added. "The roads, et cetera."

"Right, the whole layout."

They arrived in Newbridge and Bar cruised the streets around the Bluebird Motel. Dr. Lyme and The Private got out at a seafood restaurant, where they'd have dinner. Bar and Andrew proceeded to the motel, where they'd check in and have a pizza delivered. Lyme and The Private would check in separately, thus making the Talons less conspicuous as a group. This was their usual practice, in keeping with their goals of minimum visibility and zero detectability.

"So far, so good," said Andrew in the room.

"Yeah," Bar answered, "but this place is kind of hokey, don't you think?"

"You mean that manager or owner living here, her place right behind the desk?"

"Yeah, and that other business they have in back, the trucks and trailers and shit."

Andrew shrugged.

"It's not neat and impersonal like we're used to, but we can adjust. Avoid them till checkout. Maybe just leave the keys in the room. No personal contact."

Bar smiled reflectively.

"Sounds good. Yeah, I'm good at that."

Andrew wasn't sure what he meant.

"You mean, when you're at your job?"

"Yeah, there too. It's okay, though. I'm on the night shift."

They both worked in the social services, though on different levels. Andrew had an MSW and was a school counselor, while Bar lacked the professional degree and did mostly clerical work.

"Well," Andrew said, "you do what you have to, whether the 'profession' likes it or not. In the end, you can't help anyone else unless you first help yourself."

Bar nodded as he unpacked his things. They weren't quite in sync with each other, Andrew thought, despite their shared field of work. It disappointed him. Maybe his greater role in the Talons had something to do with it.

"Want me to call for the pizza?" Bar asked.

"Sure. Just so you get some vegetables on it."

"Hey, my girlfriend works in a health-food store."

Nothing like food to bring people together, Andrew considered. Although, whatever their perspectives on the social services, they were consistently linked by their dedication to the Talons. That's what he had to remember. Interpersonal differences, just like his long-held personal values, had to be set aside so the Talons could triumph. He felt confident Bar would agree.

"I want to share something with you, Bar," he said over his third piece of pizza.

"Besides the room and the pizza? And the driving? The Private might call you a communist."

"He just might. But this isn't material. No economics involved. It's a moral or just spiritual value, or concept: the thing we used to have in the Talons about no killing."

Bar eyed him steadily but kept chewing.

"Yeah, no assaults at all. No injuries, at least to humans."

"I liked it, you know? The appreciation of life—its shortness, its value. The respect for another's existence. Sympathy for pain, distress. The idea was, if we killed or assaulted, we weren't any better than our adversaries."

"Uh-huh. But it seems that was unrealistic. We were using bombs, fire. It's like expecting an army to show surgical precision."

"I guess so. But we're moving along, now. The deaths or injuries won't be accidental. And they won't be animals, like last time."

"What are you saying? You think it might be wrong, this project we're on?"

"No. I'm thinking killing is wrong, but it's justified here by the target's actions."

Bar nodded, Andrew sensing he'd made a connection.

"Yeah," said Bar, "killing is justified a lot in society, even leaving out the wars. Self-defense, suicide, removing life supports, abortion maybe. Prob'ly a lot of mercy killing done in secret."

"Then there's capital punishment."

"Right. That's what we're into *here,* isn't it?"

"Yes. Basically an execution, but more important for the message it sends. The target supports actions and policies that cause widespread suffering, but his death will also serve notice to others."

"Make an example of him."

"And let the others know we're around. They've been using the media to enforce the corporate line on war and domestic issues. Our action says stop it or else."

"Next time it might be you."

"Right."

"I like it. Yeah, I think we've justified it."

Andrew smiled in agreement, though he found Bar's conclusion prosaic. Maybe he was being ironic, never having doubted for an instant the justness of their action. But Andrew was pleased that he'd raised the issue, it had been processed, and they both could proceed without hindrance of conscience.

"Of course," Bar said, "there's the pilot."

Andrew hesitated, the term "collateral damage" coming to mind. This was a consideration they couldn't afford. They'd come too far.

"He knows what he assists in," Andrew said, "and he's no

doubt been well paid. A mercenary, basically. We needn't be concerned about him."

It sounded cold, but Bar nodded in agreement.

"Okay by me. Want to see what's on cable?"

They retired early to accommodate the early morning rising. It was gray and misty when The Private rapped on their door, advising them it was "go time." Andrew was at the wheel as they drove out of town and through a bucolic stretch to the point. They passed a country club, golf areas, and a state park, ending up on a blunt promontory fringed with a stony beach. Beyond lay the shrouded waters of Long Island Sound. The road ran parallel to the beach but Andrew stopped the van near the furthest growth of trees and bushes. Here, with the benefit of cover, they could strike at the helicopter flying from Wingham, up the coast, to the corporate studios in New York City. Dr. Lyme and The Private, without the SAM today, proceeded into the cover while Bar acted as lookout. Andrew remained in the van, poised to drive off quickly. Though it was a mild day for winter, the dampness increased the chill that eddied along the coastline.

Sitting in the parked van, his window lowered for air, Andrew reflected on the moment. It had a spiritual quality, he and his comrades waiting in gray silence to view the evil they'd take down. And he'd play a vital role, making his relationship to the others something more than political or fraternal. This was a conflict of basic universal forces. They were clearing the way for some good, progressive power to enter the forum of public discussion. Somewhere in his mind, of course, was the little voice that continued to say, "But it's wrong to kill." What the little voice didn't know, however, or didn't care about, was that their target himself supported widespread killing and other evils. The Talons' act would therefore be a just execution, as well as something to protect humanity in the future. The corporate media had to yield some control, allow the truth about corporate hegemony to reach the eyes and ears of society.

The mechanical pulse of a helicopter rose from up the coast. Andrew tensed and peered out the open window, feeling somehow intimidated by the sound. It suddenly became much louder and its source could be seen, though blurred by fog, slicing toward New York City. It was black, quite plain, and quickly gone.

Dr. Lyme and The Private were walking briskly back to the van, talking seriously. Bar followed from his vantage point, hands in pockets and looking cold. Andrew started the van and checked that the doors were unlocked. He delayed in using the headlights to avoid attracting notice.

"We'll return to the motel," said Lyme, "by a different route, more or less roundabout. We can just pass it today and go to breakfast, but tomorrow we go in and check out. In pairs again, with an interval in-between. Just a couple of business parties hitting the rush-hour road."

"Any chance they might use a roadblock?" asked Bar.

"Not until well after we're gone. Anyway, the SAM components will be back at the point, in the bushes. We'll be clean as a church choir."

Andrew took the circuitous route prescribed by Lyme, who gave directions as he consulted a local map. Reaching the motel, they breezed on by and proceeded to a busy restaurant on the far side of town. After breakfast, Bar took the wheel and they visited a large arboretum, open year-round, where they could kill the rest of the morning.

"So," asked The Private, "what're we supposed to be now? Bird-watchers?"

Dr. Lyme chuckled.

"Not a bad idea. But no, botanists is more believable. You can refer any questions to me. Or else—"

He looked at Andrew.

"You spent a lot of time in the woods, didn't you?"

"Yeah, with my father. Hunting."

"Right. Well, that's what we're doing here, in a sense. On the trip, I mean."

Andrew nodded. Just a casual remark for Lyme, quickly forgotten by him, but striking the chord in Andrew that had nagged him since their arrival. As he'd felt misgivings while trudging in the Wisconsin woods with his father, so he was haunted by the reality of their project as he walked with Lyme.

"You know," said The Private, "this dude we're taking down, some parts of his show got nothing to do with corporate power. I mean, like celebrities on trial, or a husband killed his wife, a mom killed her kids. Shit like that."

"Uh-huh," said Dr. Lyme, "and in doing that he reflects the treatment of news by his network. By giving endless attention to tabloid stories, he and the network divert attention from real issues. Ones that are 'inconvenient' to discuss. For the owners of the network, I mean, and other corporate types and their lackeys in government."

"The network," said Andrew, "would say they broadcast those stories because people *want* them, the celebrities and such."

"News as entertainment," Bar added.

"Sad but true," acknowledged Lyme. "But who was it that *conditioned* the viewing audience to that pablum? The usual suspects, right? Dishing out months of stories about one or two killings, or a celebrity rape, while ignoring the thousands being abused by our government."

"Conditioning, yeah," said The Private. "They do that with 'American interests,' too. Like it's for *us* they bomb those weddings and hospitals in Iraq and Afghanistan. What a crock of shit!"

"Misleading terminology, yes. The corporate media passes it right along. But we're supposed to be relaxing, gents. Seems our friends the trees aren't cutting it for us."

"I saw a pool hall when we were driving," Bar ventured.

"Great," said Lyme. "We can spend the afternoon there. Work the tree sap out of our lungs."

"Get the hell out of Walden Pond," smiled The Private.

"Now, now. The place is serving its purpose: kill some

time without being conspicuous, get a little exercise. Somehow, I think Thoreau would've agreed with us."

Andrew smiled to himself. Maybe the tree sap *was* getting to someone. But, along with Bar and The Private, he offered no response. They found their van and, buying sandwiches on the way, returned to their motel. After lunch, they rotated partners while playing two-on-two at the pool hall. Of the four of them, Dr. Lyme seemed most absorbed in the games, and he showed surprising skill. Aggressive and precise, he with any partner would beat the opposing team.

"Comes from being a chiropractor," he said. "All that time bending over the treatment table. I'm used to the position."

Though Andrew was sometimes bothered by Lyme's offhandedness, he admired the man's readiness for the next day's strike. Unlike himself, Lyme was apparently past the moral considerations on taking the two lives. He was free to enjoy playing pool as if they were, in fact, computer techies on an installation. Andrew wondered whether, in having his doubts, he was being a moral elitist. Perhaps what he saw as values were simply parts of a cherished self-concept that he was loath to give up. If so, it was mere selfishness that threatened to impede him. Their project was necessary for society, vital to its development, so it was foolish and wrong to let his vanity get in the way. Andrew felt grateful to Dr. Lyme for helping him see this. Whatever their differences, he should be guided by the other's example on this project.

That evening, Andrew and Bar watched Dick Hanlon's show in their motel room. The news spinner was as arrogant as ever, oblivious to the fact that he was doing his last show. Andrew could have been amused by this, taking smug satisfaction, but instead he felt pity for the man. With a morning execution awaiting him, Hanlon persisted in his frenzied service to corrupt financial schemers. He railed against regulation, the United Nations, professors, and non-Judeo-Christians. Bar got tired of it and went to take a shower, but Andrew stayed and heard a later segment concerning the

Earth Freedom Force, from which two cells had split to join the Talons.

"Why *not* use the army against them?" insisted Hanlon. "Since local authorities can't do the job, or *won't*, give the scum a taste of *real* military force! And don't tell me about *Posse Comitatus*, Tenth Amendment, and the like. We're all Americans, aren't we? The EFF is our enemy, so send in the army!"

Andrew hit the *mute* button and watched Hanlon's mouth working silently. He'd be talking against *habeas corpus*, calling for military tribunals, but Andrew was starting to feel the nausea that had driven Bar to the shower. Still, Andrew wanted to see the show to its end, to witness Hanlon's final performance in the series that merited his death. It was a necessary ritual, since any death was an issue for Andrew and had to be fully processed.

In the morning The Private brought coffee to their room.

"Twenty minutes," he said. "Everybody okay on this?"

"I'm fine," replied Andrew.

"No problem," Bar added.

The Private nodded.

"We got good conditions. Everything's go. Me and Lyme'll be in the van. Time it to the minute."

"Right," said Andrew.

The mist was less dense than the day before, but the chill was somehow more penetrating. Maybe the caffeine, Andrew thought. He drove to the point by the same route, careful to observe all traffic laws. Nobody joked about his caution. They rode in near-silence, The Private taking SAM components out of computer boxes. As Andrew heard the sounds, he gazed over the park and golf land that lined the road, imagined how the morning's peace would soon be shattered. Not our fault, he thought. It's an extension of the shattered peace in other lands, and the shattering of lives here under arrogant policies. My daughter back home in her crib, her entire generation, depends on this action today to save our society. Some would say the *world* depends on it–the "global village"–all our destinies interconnected.

He parked the van and Bar got out to ascend his vantage point. He carried a cell phone to warn of interlopers. Once he was in place, Dr. Lyme and The Private unloaded the missile round. They each gripped the leather shoulder strap, on opposite sides, and carried it low between them. The Private cradled the gripstock in his free arm, while Dr. Lyme held the battery/cooling unit. Andrew watched as they disappeared into the furthest clump of substantial trees and bushes. From a distance, it would not have been clear what they were carrying. It could have been survey equipment or other tools. Yet, within a minute, The Private would be poised to launch a stinger.

"It's not too late," said the little voice in Andrew's mind. "You can start the motor and drive quickly away, go all the way to Wisconsin. Or dump the van en route and take a plane or train. Forget you ever heard of the Talons or the Failure Club."

But Andrew knew it couldn't happen. Besides the repercussions of such an act, he was incapable of betraying his comrades at this point. Their escape and safety were in his hands, and they were risking their lives for a cause in which he passionately believed. The little voice was just a prisoner in a chamber of his brain, desperate for power. However evil this day might appear in the abstract, what they were doing was necessary and good. Andrew could never live with himself if he ran from it, or failed to do his part.

In the distance, the thrumming of the helicopter began.

Relaxed, matter-of-fact now in his thinking, Andrew searched the skies through the van's windows. The fog at first held their quarry back, but it soon emerged in the new day's refracted light. It was oddly lacking in ugliness today, this giant insect, taking on beauty for Andrew because of its value. Of course, they had to bring it down to capture that value, so they hunted it as prize game. His father would be proud,

Andrew thought, if he could understand this hunt. But the pride would have to stay with Andrew and his comrades, though many would share in the joy of their victory.

The helicopter was before him now, farther out over the Sound than the day before. It began to pass by, as yet unmolested, and Andrew felt a flicker of panic. It was only for an instant, though, because the next moment was filled with flame and a thunderclap that rattled the van. Amid smoke that blocked all else from view, the twisted remains of the helicopter turned toward the water below. It fell slowly, as if held up by the heavenward motion of the flames. Andrew drank in the spectacle with a blank mind, entranced by the horror and vague glory, failing for a time to function. But then he saw the others jogging towards the van.

"Go! Go! Go! Go!" barked The Private getting in, and Andrew shot away, soon relaxing to inconspicuous speed.

"Perfect," Dr. Lyme declared. "That was perfect. Good work, men."

"We ain't outta here yet," objected The Private.

"We'll be okay."

Andrew glanced over at him. There was solemnity in Lyme, a junking of his usual brashness. Perhaps he was only now aware of the gravity of their act.

"Okay there, Bar?"

"No problem, Doc."

Surprisingly few people had been roused by the explosion, and some of them were gazing at utility lines and intersections to find the source. There was eventually a police siren, but by then the Talons were approaching their motel.

"Be sure to leave a tip," said Dr. Lyme, "but not too big. We don't want them to remember us either way."

He looked tired later as they left town. Despite their efforts to be smooth and put their feelings aside, Andrew realized, the project had been a drain on them. It was utterly different from when they had sabotaged only property. To kill someone, no matter whom, left you in a radically changed relationship with society. You had assumed the ultimate authority, foregoing innocence, and could no longer claim moral purity. You were forever defective as a human being. And yet it had been necessary to kill Hanlon and the drive against corporate power must continue. For the sake of today's societies and the future, the Talons for Earth Freedom had to give from their very souls. With Bar at the wheel, they were well into Pennsylvania before anyone thought about breakfast. Even then, it was just Bar and The Private who ate, Andrew and the doctor opting to ruminate over their coffee.

CHAPTER 7

Surrounded by the sunlit early spring of the Rocky Mountains, three United States soldiers sat imprisoned in a converted smokehouse. They'd been seized over 100 miles away while enjoying themselves in a town near their base. Their abductors were a contingent from the Talons for Earth Freedom, a growing organization of social militants. The smokehouse prison was part of a compound nestled amid dense woods, reached by a rough dirt road, and devoid of utility lines. The Talons and their prisoners were thus cut off from the outside world, except when the militants in charge chose to communicate. They'd do this through the proven method of a video showing the abject prisoners. The usual hooded guards would appear, weapons at hand, thus maximizing the effect and the Talons' power.

One of the leaders of the project, known as Brother's Boy, had watched the production of the video from the main house. He was a tall, heavy man with bushy hair and a nondescript beard. He smiled unconsciously as his co-leader, Blue Pond, directed the action in the clearing. She moved assertively, using aggressive gestures with both the prisoners and her fellow Talons. She couldn't be in the video herself, since her small stature would be a clue for the enemy, so Brother's Boy let her be the boss instead. Although she was a militant progressive, he thought, she still wanted to be a movie star as much as other women. Failing that, she'd accept more power. And he didn't mind yielding some to her. He had enough to do running the camp and the operation, and most of all in deciding the fate of the prisoners.

Each of the leaders had once headed a cell in the Earth Freedom Force, which was environmental in focus. But after they combined for an attack on a mining company, resulting in injuries and a brief kidnapping, they found themselves ostracized. They were soon contacted by a shadowy network of militants that arranged their alliance with the Talons of the Phoenix, a group to the east that was looking to expand. Two members of the former Phoenix group were among the hooded guards in the video directed by Blue Pond. This was deeply satisfying to Brother's Boy, since he could believe now that they had strength in numbers and higher leadership would support him. He needn't rely only on a frail Canadian girl for help in fighting the corporate giants. She'd contributed her energy and her people, but she lacked a clear understanding of effective political violence.

"Will we be killing them, then?" she asked.

"That wasn't the reason we took them."

"Well, we can't hold them forever. One is a woman, in that same little space with two men."

Brother's Boy laughed.

"One minute you're talking about killing, the next you're concerned about mixed company."

She gave him a petulant look. Her face was small with delicate features except for her deep, dark eyes, glaring from the cover of her straight, black hair, cropped short for combat.

"Anyway," he continued, "the video first arrives tomorrow. We need to see the reaction."

"Then make our demands?"

"They'll handle it from the Midwest, if there *are* demands. Andrew wasn't sure how they'd play it."

"Which leaves us dangling here, choice bait for rescue ops."

"Oh, I'm sure there's a plan. But at a higher level than Andrew, so he doesn't know it."

Blue Pond looked off into the night sky. Brother's Boy followed her gaze to the imposing canopy of stars that lit the mountainside. They were on the porch of the main house, the other Talons inside or in the outbuildings. There was no fire in the camp since it would compromise their safety.

"In the end, of course," said Blue Pond, "it's up to you. Whatever the plans on high, you're in charge here and can do what you want. Those far away will accept your explanation."

Brother's Boy shifted uncomfortably.

"We're both in charge here, Blue."

"You know they listen to you more, even my own group. You're the man."

He looked at her but had no response. He gripped her arm in reassurance, but was amazed again by its smallness. He'd never questioned her authority, knowing its roots in her exploited life in Alberta. Her parents were essentially servants at the resorts, where she'd had a second-class childhood under the eyes of the wealthy. A bit to the east the oil fields bloomed, a garden of profit for the powerful near and far. That she should head a cell of militants was natural, but Brother's Boy knew there were limits to such authority. To lead protracted operations you needed more than resentment and the will to act. It required a tough sort of patience, the ability to wait the enemy out and then compromise to gain concessions. He suspected it was a "gender thing." Women could reject violence or lash out suddenly, but the gradual, strategic use of force was a province of males.

Brother's Boy himself had grown up in northern California. He was sent to private schools and was passing at Stanford when he suddenly dropped out. His family and most of his friends were mystified, but they hadn't appreciated what was gnawing at him. He'd increasingly seen himself taking a common route for his economic class, one that rounded the corners of the individual and molded him as a soldier of commerce. He'd watched the changes in his father, a corporate lawyer, as he'd grown up. The spontaneous, affectionate man of his childhood had evolved into a cliché-prone, morally confused tool. At the high school, though it was run by a religious order, Brother's Boy and his classmates were groomed to follow their fathers in the corporate—and perhaps military—wars, returning some booty to the school. One of them had broken from the herd, however, and now commanded this camp with imprisoned American soldiers.

"So," said Blue Pond, "how do you think it'll end?"

"Like I said, we have to wait on developments."

"I meant later, Bro. After all the projects. We're not going to be Talons for Earth Freedom forever, right? Assuming we live long, I mean."

Brother's Boy nodded, gazing into the dark.

"Well, a movement has to resolve itself within a limited time. Otherwise it's written off as impossible. Like Marxism, and maybe peace in the Middle East. They won't stamp us out. We're on the rise and our network expands internationally. Who knows how far? On the other hand, we're not going to wipe out corporations or take over the U.S. government. So it ends, I guess, when we get enough out of them, or when we control them enough to prevent major abuses."

One of the Talons from the Midwest, known as Sludge, came out onto the porch. Tall and strongly built, he had a menacing look due to his overhanging brows.

"Beautiful night," he remarked.

"More or less typical," said Brother's Boy. "Lots of beauty at this altitude."

"Away from mankind," Blue Pond added.

Sludge smiled over at her.

"Aren't *we* mankind?"

She was silent but Brother's Boy turned to him.

"We're mankind plus. A fast-forward in the masses' consciousness. Without our guests over there, we'd be at one with all this."

His arm swept toward the stars.

"I like it," Sludge responded. "And, I'll tell you, I like it out *here*, in the West. I wouldn't mind staying after the gig."

"Aren't there people who would miss you?" asked Blue Pond. "Who *you* would miss?"

"Personal relationships. Yeah, maybe. But hey, they come and go anyway. Like a guy told me once, it's all propinquity. All you can do is be in the right place. That's most important. Then relate as you will with whoever's there. Whatever you have in your favorite place, that's the best you can do."

"There can be problems in a favorite place," said Blue Pond.

Sludge hesitated.

"Yeah, that's right."

His deep-set eyes searched the darkness, his lips suddenly sealed. Brother's Boy had noticed this about him earlier, his splashes of expressiveness that dropped into moody oblivion.

"What about your partner?" he asked. "Does he share your feelings?"

"Derek? No, he's an inner-city guy. Doesn't have to go as far for more space. Out here is like another planet for him."

Blue Pond excused herself and went in the house.

"Did I say something wrong?"

Brother's Boy laughed it off.

"No, she's got things to do. We're all under some strain, I think, with the prisoners here. It isn't in our natures to imprison—even less than it is to kill. But it's part of the sacrifice we make to reach our greater goals. Our personal values—desires, too—have to stay in cold storage so the Talons can triumph."

Sludge nodded in agreement.

"Of course," he said.

They both looked out into the night as sounds of a card game rose from the house behind them.

• • •

The sun was near zenith, the day unseasonably warm, as most of the Talons idled about the camp. Brother's Boy was taking a call on his cell phone, learning of an attack on a weapons plant in Georgia that morning. It was somehow the work of the Talons, although the caller, Andrew, said that no one from his Midwest group was involved. The overall head of the Talons, Dr. Xyntius, had only given a vague explanation. A supporter of the Talons in Canada, where their connections were murky, had personally established a branch around Atlanta, recruiting a radical discussion group. In their initial effort, the new Talons had blown up the offices of a warplane supplier, and part of one of their factories as well.

"There were some injuries," said Andrew, "apparently unavoidable. No deaths. We'll be claiming responsibility in time for the evening news. Their biggest customer is the DOD, so we'll get the max reaction, red alert and all. You guys will be included—it'll be seen as connected to your action—so you need to clean things up *today*. We can't make any demands just now, so it's time to disappear, maintain invisibility."

"And the prisoners? Any word from Dr. X on *them*?"

"He's making that your call. If you can release them unharmed, it should help our credibility, show we're not after the little guy. On the other hand, if you can't dump them safely, well, we have to think of our operatives first, and our undetectability."

"It won't be easy in the daytime. We'll need to carry them quite a ways, avoid any tie-in with the camp."

"Time is short, yes. But like I say, if you can't make it with a live cargo, I'm sure the backers will understand."

Brother's Boy was irritated. Andrew, he knew, had his own issues with the taking of lives, even those of animals. It was a basis for respect between them. Now, though, they could only react to events caused by those higher up. For Andrew, it meant making this call. For Brother's Boy, it meant hastening a decision that was already difficult. He told Andrew he'd take care of it, later realizing that he'd forgotten Blue Pond. Granted, she was struggling with her identity as a leader. But no one was challenging her, including him, so she should share in the decision-making on this. He decided to confer with her before giving any orders.

Not finding her in the house, he went out into the camp. A number of Talons were standing in the middle of the clearing, watching Derek demonstrate karate moves. Brother's Boy noticed that Sludge, Derek's fellow Midwesterner, was not among the observers. Everything else appeared normal, both here and among the outbuildings, with no one showing a sense of urgency such as Brother's Boy felt.

"Anybody here seen Blue Pond?" he asked.

The Talons hesitated, for some reason glancing at Derek. The karate had raised a light sweat that glistened beneath his Afro.

"She went to check an approach path in the woods," he said. "Took Sludge along as escort."

"I see."

One or two of the others shifted uncomfortably. Brother's Boy tried to ignore them, keeping his eyes on Derek.

"We'll be moving out soon. We all need to get things together, close the buildings. Derek, I need you to be with Maki when he brings out the prisoners."

"Sure, man. Soon as I grab my gear. You want someone should go get Blue Pond?" A hesitation. "And Sludge?"

"No, I'll do it myself. I know the path."

He left them and headed for the smokehouse prison. Maki, a short, husky man with a large gun in his belt, watched him approach. Maki was always alert, always ready to kill, an unfortunate necessity for militant social activists.

"We're moving out," Brother's Boy told him. "Derek is

coming to help with the prisoners. Move them into the yard in full restraints."

"Right," said Maki. Then quickly, "Blue know about it? She said we should wait her orders."

Maki was from Blue Pond's cell. More than her other members, he'd reserved his primary loyalty for her.

"I'm going to get her now," Brother's Boy answered. "Shit came down from the Midwest. Higher command says wrap it up, so we go *today*."

He was moving toward the woods while still talking, letting Maki know the conversation was over. He hadn't said what they would do with the prisoners, and he actually didn't know. He wanted to release them, but there were suddenly too many variables in the situation. He wouldn't commit himself to a quick decision. He needed the input of a co-leader, the role he'd been confident Blue Pond could fill. But as he picked his way along the mountain path, inured to the charms of early wildflowers, he sensed that he was alone in deciding the soldiers' fate, that Blue Pond was a fatalistic illusion of leadership.

She still worked at the Alberta resorts between operations. He'd drifted to Oregon, where he had a small business cleaning windows and roof gutters. He inwardly recoiled from the cycle of employment and consumerism that gripped his peers. He watched as it devoured their time, warped their perspectives, instilled the values of corporate America. They were squeezed or cajoled for the maximum profits, usually not breaking but also never secure enough to think or act independently. In Blue Pond he'd found an enlightened woman, someone who appreciated their cause in a broader sense than their operatives did. She was an answer to the solitude he felt as leader, as well as a buffer against banal conversation. Still, she'd advanced as he had from separateness to alienation, and without his company might have drifted too far, which was a form of failure since it discouraged action. As it was—or so he wanted to believe, they were enabling each other to reenter society as part of its power structure, not through a corporate ideology but through selective force and reason.

He hadn't seen them yet, wondered why they weren't in the open. There was an inviting little niche he'd noticed the other day, shady with a clear running stream. He decided to check it out and wondered further: Why Sludge? With all the Talons she'd known longer, why pick him as her escort? Despite the urgency of Brother's Boy's quest, he slowed his walk.

He approached the niche softly, invisibly, instinctively knowing they were there. The quiet rise and fall of her slim brown torso came as no surprise. He saw her from behind, rising above a latticework of foliage. She was dappled with sunlight as she moved, a smiling sun tattoo winking at him from her shoulder. She gasped and sighed, while a low grunt rose occasionally from below. Brother's Boy forgot for a moment the crisis at the camp, corporate hegemony and its corollary issues, and everything else, seeing all his meaning in the rise and fall of Blue Pond's back. He was suddenly, he saw, very close to defeat in life. Refusing to seal his own destruction, he retreated from the niche even more softly than he'd approached.

He stood back on the path with hands on hips, aware again of the jingoes who controlled government on behalf of commercial despots. Aware again of the glorification of the military, of which three hapless members were his prisoners. Aware again of indifference to torture, feel-good religion with its callous dictates, the corruption of the two-party system. He saw the masses with their fear of the inner self, fear of differing with group suggestion, fear of losing their ration of security in the competitive, materialistic society. He saw himself, standing among wildflowers, his buffer against the chaos dissolving in a nearby niche.

There were shots in the direction of the camp. Two, then no more. Possibly hunters, Brother's Boy thought, then knew he was in denial. He had to act, and at once, as a leader of the Talons for Earth Freedom. This despite his failure—his inability—to accomplish his purpose out here on the path.

They were quickly behind him, however, Sludge less skilled than Blue Pond at rapid dressing. Brother's Boy ignored his dishevelment.

"We're moving out," he said. "And something's gone wrong."

They ran as best they could along the uneven path, Sludge discreetly trailing the two leaders.

...

Ilena, an ambulance worker and one of Brother's Boy's Talons, was attending to a wounded prisoner on the ground. The vans and car were standing open, gear partially loaded, while the other Talons surrounded the prisoners and Ilena. From where Brother's Boy entered the camp, it appeared none of them had been injured. Maki and a couple of others were holding guns. The prisoners had been blindfolded.

"This one slipped a restraint," Maki explained, "went for my gun. It went off in the struggle. Jacoby had a shot and stopped it."

Jacoby, tall with tousled hair, nodded when Brother's Boy turned to him.

"Good work not to kill him," said the leader.

"He can't make us," added Maki. "We had our half-masks on."

The thigh wound, though apparently not life-threatening, had drawn a lot of blood.

"He can't be moved a long ways," said Ilena. "Shouldn't be, anyway." There was a waver in her voice, anxiety in the bounce of her pony tail.

She knows we have a new problem, Brother's Boy thought, and so do the others. Glancing at Blue Pond, he saw that her jaw was set, her stare hard at the prisoners. She'd be for killing them, he knew, were it not for the incident in the woods. She has to hold back now from that kind of authority.

At least while Sludge is around, and until she's sure again of my support. He noticed Derek moving to his side.

"Hey, man. I want to say I'm sorry. I shoulda stopped him without the dude having to shoot. You want to tell Andrew I fucked up, I'll understand."

"No," said Brother's Boy quickly, "I don't blame you a bit. We appreciate your help, Sludge's too. Any report will be full-bred positive. Only I want you two out of here on the first vehicle. We have to protect the connection between our parts of the organization. We can't have you found with us if it comes to that."

"Right, man. He'll get his bag and we're ready to split."

Brother's Boy again surveyed the scene. He had Blue Pond's option if he wanted it, and the argument for it was strong. Three dead bodies were easily transported and could be dumped undiscovered for as long as they wanted. His own preference, releasing them alive at a distant location, was now eliminated. They were pressed for time, having even less now than when Andrew had called. All he knew for sure, standing in the sun with an armed band waiting his decision, was that he didn't want to kill but was committed to immediate social progress. If there was no real alternative, his personal values must be set aside.

"We have to move," Blue Pond ventured.

"I know," he answered.

He almost asked her to trust him, lend her tacit support, but then realized he had to seize the moment, speak with absolute authority. Only then would the Talons proceed with full confidence, make something work and get everyone out safely. Taking most of the group out of earshot of the prisoners, he dictated his plan as it appeared before him.

"We'll drop off our guests in Red Pine," he said. "It's the first sizable town past Jonaston, where we got some groceries. We'll leave them on the shady side of a church, one that's closed with nothing going on. They'll be in full restraints. We'll make a call an hour later in case they're still sitting."

He led them back to the prisoners. The wounded man was barely conscious. The other male prisoner was struggling to be stoic, while the woman was clearly devastated. Within himself, Brother's Boy admired the semi-stoic soldier. But he also pitied the misplaced loyalty that had led these three to his clutches—to possible execution for the sins of rulers and corporate vermin.

"Prisoners," he said, "you will soon be released, but only if you fully cooperate with the transportation and drop-off. Any further resistance from any of you and *all three* will be killed immediately."

He glanced at Blue Pond, who was standing at his side. She was glaring at the prisoners with a slight smile. Satisfied, Brother's Boy thought.

"Show your gratitude when you return," he continued. "Remember, we could have killed you at any time. Explain that we're a humane organization fighting for the common people against fascist dictates and corporate exploitation. Look at your families, friends, communities. See what's happening to them under the present order, as well as to all society and throughout the world. Then you may judge us. Then you will *join* us!"

He turned back to the Talons and drew them away again from the prisoners. He began grouping people for the vehicles, explaining details of the departure trip, sending people on tasks. He noticed Blue Pond walking away toward the main house with Maki. Getting her gear, he thought. But he also sensed her drifting further into the margins of the operation. Despite the spectacle in the woods, he wasn't ready to accept that. There was a crisis at hand, yes, and he was handling it, but there were unknown crises in the struggle ahead for which he'd need every resource he could muster. Chief among those, he continued to believe, was Blue Pond, for himself and so also for the movement. It wasn't logical—he'd had his doubts, they'd been confirmed—but he knew that he needed that spirit in her that had attracted and inspired others. He couldn't let her be marginalized.

He headed for the main house as soon as he could break away. He found that Maki had packed his things and was gathering those of Blue Pond, who was finishing a shower. She came out wearing a hotel bathrobe.

"We need to talk," Brother's Boy told her.

"I'll take care of the smokehouse," said Maki. He was quickly gone. Blue Pond continued the packing, setting aside a fresh set of clothes for the departure.

"I guess this is about the woods," she said.

"No," he answered, but it sounded tentative. "Not exactly."

"What, then?"

"About our future."

She looked at him fully, her dark eyes wide with anticipation. He'd meant the future of the Talons, their western operations, but Blue Pond was responding to something nearer—here, in this room. She glanced toward the activity outside.

"Do you think this is the time, Bro? I mean—"

"It's the very best time."

She viewed him from several paces away, a smile beginning on her lips. Her hair was still wet, combed straight down all around.

"The very best?"

"Yes. There's the drop-off of the prisoners. I was thinking you could supervise it, take whoever you want with you."

She hesitated, tilting her head.

"I thought you were taking charge. You looked really great out there. To everyone."

"It's important they remember we're co-leaders, we work as equals and they relate to us that way."

She began to bow her head, but quickly recovered.

"Yeah, I agree. Thanks, Bro. I appreciate the confidence. Especially—well, of *course* I want to do the drop."

"Good."

She turned toward the clothes she'd laid out, casually sliding off the robe and casting it aside. Her lean body was well browned by a lifetime of nude swimming. Brother's Boy had seen her like this before, so what first caught his eye was the smiling sun tattoo on her shoulder. It began to raise a memory of the woods, but Blue Pond cancelled it by turning toward him with hands on hips, feet spread purposefully.

"That is," she said, "if you're sure you can trust me—this *woman* you see before you."

She sucked in her stomach, raising her small breasts a bit, accentuating her pudenda.

"Like you say," she continued softly, "it's the future that counts. Starting with the rest of today, but going on to when there's no more Talons. For all that time, Bro, I want you to know you're number one for me, just like you were out there."

She waved toward the clearing, alerting him again to the crisis. He stepped up to her and gripped her shoulder above the smiling sun.

"I trust you fully," he said, "now and for later, as long as you want." A hesitation. "I need you, Blue."

She looked at his hand on her shoulder.

"Five minutes," she said, "and I'll be right out."

CHAPTER 8

Following a shakeup at the Department of Homeland Security, a massive investigation was launched to find the Talons for Earth Freedom. Agents were pulled from ongoing and uncompleted assignments to focus on the suddenly emerged top domestic threat. Within about half a year, the Talons had been responsible for at least five attacks that had dominated the news. The first two, almost benign in retrospect, were the simultaneous killings of prize animals belonging to an environmental official and a chemical magnate. This was followed by the downing of a helicopter containing the leading conservative news spinner on television. More recently, the Talons had kidnapped three soldiers near their domestic base, releasing them after displaying them in a video. One of the soldiers had a gunshot wound. Overlapping this action was an attack on the offices and plant of a warplane producer, resulting in extensive damage that stalled operations.

Agent DeWitte Gormer had been reassigned from his scrutiny of posters and bumper stickers hostile to the president. He'd joined Homeland Security after a brief stint as a suburban patrolman, which he found intolerably boring. Since his B.A.

was in liberal arts, however, his best move was to something else in law enforcement. Spotting the new positions related to terrorism, he jumped through the hoop of opportunity. He now found himself with a new partner, Yvonne Billups, fresh from infiltrating churches that raised money to help war victims. Though she hadn't finished college, she'd worked several years as an airport screener and thus qualified to investigate terrorism. Yvonne was a decade older then DeWitte, and had a son who stayed with his grandmother when Yvonne traveled on assignments.

"We'll pair you up," the assistant director had said, "for maximum access to a variety of personalities. Partners will therefore tend to differ according to race, gender, age group, and other characteristics."

Each team of agents was assigned a suspicious organization to investigate. DeWitte and Yvonne received a Level C, or low priority, file on the Failure Club. It was ostensibly a social organization for losers that recruited via the Internet. However, its membership included a number of people with criminal records or less-than-honorable military discharges. Others in the club were identified as respected professionals in various fields. None were known to have terrorist ties, but the odd mix warranted a closer look. In the current climate of fear of domestic terrorism, a couple of lesser-skilled agents could be spared to confirm the group's innocence. The eventual report could be filed in the agents' records as a training exercise, thus helping to meet staff development goals.

"Before closing your investigation," said the assistant director, "you need to make substantial and sufficient contacts."

DeWitte and Yvonne were foiled on their first attempted interview, wasting time and government gas in rural West Virginia. Their would-be contact, Hugo Smetters a.k.a. Bo, was a long-distance trucker currently on the road. Since his wife claimed "I don't know nothing" about the Failure Club, the agents were soon back on the road themselves.

"She prob'ly doesn't *want* to know anything," said Yvonne, "considering what he might be doing out there."

She glared out the passenger window past her ebony arm, which rested in the frame as she held a cigarette. She wore her black hair in large curls complemented by silver hoop earrings.

"I'd guess he's in the habit of not telling her much," said DeWitte. "A club meeting seems innocent enough, but it might connect up to other 'adventures.'"

He had short reddish hair, balding in front, and a long oval face that watched the road calmly, almost sleepily. He wore a cheap suit.

"Well, at least we got started," said Yvonne. "We made a contact."

"Yeah, it's a start. I don't know about 'substantial and sufficient.'"

"Hey, we're following his procedure, recommendation or whatever. Peck away at the edges, he said, work your way in."

"'Peripheral focus,' I think he said. Advance to the center like a slow flame—like a cancer, maybe."

She looked at him with eyes narrowed.

"You don't have to put it *that* way!" And she blew some smoke back toward the window.

The assistant director had told them to start with lesser members of their groups and outside contacts of the bigger fish. In this way, an organization would not pick up as quickly on their scrutiny. The membership as a whole would not clam up too soon.

"There's one of our beautiful one-stars coming up," said Yvonne.

"You want to let that student go till tomorrow?"

"Hell, yes. I'm not traipsing into some dorm or frat house. Not during drinking hours, anyway. We have the boy's class schedule. So, hit him tomorrow."

DeWitte smiled but didn't laugh. Yvonne seemed all right, trustworthy and someone who'd pull her weight, but there wasn't the natural rapport he'd had with his previous partner.

Llewellyn had also been his senior, but with him it had yielded a guided tour of the world's seamy pleasures. They'd be stopping to pick up a bottle about now, or looking forward to a topless bar. They'd cruise a town they entered to find the hottest prospect for kicks that night. Their crackdown on the president's enemies became grist for jokes, or was dismissed with contempt.

He thought of his old partner again as he sat in his motel room. Llewellyn had received a Level B file and a new male partner, headed for the West Coast, and was no doubt enjoying himself. By contrast, DeWitte was navigating the channels on a barely operative television, the sound muted against irritating show and commercial fragments. He could hear Yvonne in the next room, talking long-distance with her son. Was this to be their nightly routine, then? He might as well be a suburban cop again, sitting by himself in the marked car, waiting hour after hour for something to happen. "The patrol boy," they started to call him. Irritation welled up, threatened to become rage. The remote and the TV screen were in danger of violent contact. DeWitte was relieved when Yvonne came over, holding the file with its wealth of potential interviews.

"The way I see it," she said, "we catch Alain early tomorrow at the college, then move west toward Indiana. We can hit these two on the way, Tom and Mary Ellen, maybe on the same stop. A twofer."

"Yes, they share an address. But she has a second one, too. A nurse's residence?"

"Yeah. Funny someone her age should keep a room there. Guess Mr. Hartigan must have his moods. He was a general discharge. Goes by 'The Private' in the club."

"Oh, boy."

"Yeah, well, they're on the way. We'd be swinging up then toward this area past Indy. The place they usually meet is there, a retreat center run by monks."

"The vice-president's town is just off the highway. Judge Martin Waters. He's up in years, I see. Chances are he's conservative—a friendly contact."

Yvonne shrugged.

"I dunno. 'Peripheral focus' and all. Though he's not involved on the website, or in business matters or public relations."

"We can think about it."

"Okay. And what about this guy?"

There was a new inflection to her voice and DeWitte saw she was smiling.

"'Lloyd Henry Streughol,'" he read, "'a.k.a. Megadamus. Professional psychic.' Now *that* would win the stamp of incompetence! A nice big dent in each of our careers!"

"Say no more," she chuckled. "We'll pass on the great Megadamus, catch his act another time."

"Though we still have those monks to deal with. 'Galactic Retreat Center.' Wow!"

"No avoiding that one. Their meeting place, where it all begins—whatever 'it' might be. 'Substantial and sufficient,' here we come!"

They decided to head north after the monks to interview Marlena, a realtor, and then cross into Michigan to see Mrs. Xyntius, wife of the club's president. This last, more aggressive plan gave DeWitte pause. Level C file or not, he was now into something more challenging than anti-administration bumper stickers. Imagining again the times with Llewellyn, he suddenly felt tired. But Yvonne was still energized, faintly amused as she flipped through the file. Perhaps she sensed opportunity. He'd have to go along with her, he saw, on most of what she wanted. She was the senior agent and more world-wise. Unfortunately, she was also given to dull evenings polluted with work issues.

• • •

On the campus of Weisbrodt College, they pulled Alain Douz out of his human anatomy lab for questioning. Since

Yvonne was leery of the cadavers, DeWitte had to make a single-agent approach to the professor and Alain, displaying his badge to the amusement of the students. Alain, tall and slender with dark hair and moustache, went with the agents to a vacant classroom. He readily acknowledged his membership in the Failure Club, and that he'd attended meetings.

"I don't get it," said Yvonne. "A fine young man like you, a pre-med student. Why do you want to hang with failure types?"

"I joined because of Dr. Xyntius," Alain responded. "He was once on the faculty here. Then he had his presidential campaign, the Relativity Party. I guess people see him as—you know, flakey. But I don't know. I kind of like the idea of applying scientific principles to government. When I heard he had an organization, I wanted to check it out. The name didn't affect me."

"Have you seen or heard anything suspicious at the meetings?" asked DeWitte.

"Suspicious? No, it's just a club. Social, supportive. They get group discounts on travel and things, but I haven't taken advantage. Too many school expenses."

"What about politics? Same line as the election?"

"No, not really. They take votes on whether to support isolated causes. But there's no particular ideology running through them."

"Doesn't seem very scientific," said Yvonne.

"I guess Dr. Xyntius loosened up on that. He lost the election, after all."

The investigators were soon finished with Alain. He returned to the lab as Yvonne lit a cigarette in the classroom.

"So," she said, "what do you think?"

"Seems like a good kid."

"Kid, huh? Spoken by the wizened old agent."

"Okay. I mean he's a contact for our report but not much else. No inside information."

"Maybe none exists."

"Okay by me. It'll make our job easier, a *lot* easier."

As they approached their car, DeWitte hesitated and twirled the vehicle's keys.

"Would you like to drive awhile?"

"No, that's okay, baby. You're doing fine."

"'Baby'?"

"Oh, loosen up, Agent Gormer!"

He smiled and took his seat behind the wheel. She was right, he knew. It was looseness of a different sort that had helped him work with Llewellyn. Now he had to accommodate Yvonne, let *her* personal style grease the gears of investigation.

As they neared Columbus, they exited the highway and sought the residence of Tom Hartigan, a.k.a. The Private, and Mary Ellen Boruff. It was well outside the listed town, down a gravel road off the blacktop, then a dirt track through trees and thick undergrowth. A short way in, a wooden sign was suspended on poles above the track. It read "FROM MY COLD DEAD HANDS," with a crude sketch of them holding a gun. A smaller sign stated that the property was insured by a gun company, followed by a hanging dummy labeled "trespasser." As the barking of several large dogs began, DeWitte slowed the car to a crawl, then stopped.

At first not looking at Yvonne, he reflected on his situation. Did the salary he made justify this degree of risk? Was he really "dedicated," or was he looking for steppingstones over the trouble spots?

"We have the alternate address," he ventured.

"Back it out slowly," Yvonne replied.

Despite her directive, he accelerated as he neared the road, then sprayed some gravel as he shot away from the entrance. They were well clear before they spoke.

"Another 'not home'?" DeWitte asked.

"No, we never went there. Just made a wrong turn. Shit, we don't need to get our heads blown off! One interview's as good as another."

She dug in her purse and was soon relaxing with a cigarette. They continued on to Columbus and soon arrived at the hospital where Mary Ellen worked. Gratefully parking in the non-threatening venue, the agents collected themselves so they'd again exude authority. They were directed from the nurses' residence to Mary Ellen's duty floor in the hospital, where they found her busily engaged. She was slightly stocky with gray-flecked brown hair. The agents had to talk with her at the nurses' station.

"The club doesn't really do much for me," she said. "I go to be supportive of Tom. He likes going to the meetings, voting on things, hanging out later. It gives his life some structure. Most of the club's plans don't go anywhere, of course. It's the *Failure* Club. But maybe seeing that other people fail, that even a group fails, is therapeutic for the members. They *do* get group discounts on things, but that's all handled by one or two of the officers."

"Which ones?" queried Yvonne.

"Dr. Lyme, the secretary, makes some of the contacts. But in the end they're all handled by the treasurer, Mr. Singh."

Mary Ellen was approached by another nurse. As they conferred, a phone rang and Mary Ellen answered it. DeWitte leaned in close to Yvonne's ear.

"She's been pretty straightforward. Think we have enough?"

"Yeah, she's clean. The club, too. We'll keep shopping for contacts, though, make a nice report. Right now I'm for lunch."

After they'd left, Mary Ellen asked an aide to watch the station. She proceeded to a stairway and down one floor, where she used a public phone at the end of the hall.

"Yes," she spoke into the receiver, "they were here. You'd better contact Dr. Lyme right away."

• • •

As DeWitte drove toward Indianapolis, he and Yvonne

respected each other's gloom over their last interview. A surprised caretaker had shown them to where Judge Waters sat in the garden behind his house. A straw hat shaded his aged features amid the scents of new May flowers.

"I'm not staying here," he said. "Shipping out for the Orient next week. I swim there in a pond full of lotuses. Come up from the bottom and spread'em like a curtain."

"We'd like to talk with you about the Failure Club," DeWitte stated.

"You bring doughnuts? There was no black bread this morning. Had to bat her around a little." A head jerk toward the caretaker. "Can't have that, no black bread."

"Sir," said Yvonne, "we understand you're the vice-president of the organization. The Failure Club, I mean. Do you understand?"

"Yes, well, I had a defendant once. He'd come in yelling 'Hot balls for sale! Hot balls for sale!'" The judge chuckled. "Guess it's the same old story: If you got a hunch, bet a bunch! Say, how many corners on a roundhouse?"

He tapped DeWitte's leg with his cane.

"I don't know," the agent responded. "How many?"

"Don't know myself. Haven't figured it out yet. We go way back, you know. Colonel Emery served with the Confederacy. Bathed the family name in glory. Let's see, that was on the Kentucky side and—"

"Excuse me, sir," said Yvonne. "Are you feeling all right? Do you understand what we're saying to you?"

"No, I never liked L.A. Too many shylocks there. Every time you turn around, there's one on your ass. My wife, now, my *late* wife—you know, she appeared to me the other day. She—say, you look younger than me!"

He was fixing DeWitte with an amazed look.

"I'm not going to stay here, you know. I'm shipping out next week for the Orient. Gonna swim up from the bottom of the pond, spread the lotuses like a curtain!"

They'd left with their methodology fully frustrated. In the

car now, DeWitte decided to break the silence.

"I'd say that clinches it," he said. "It must be a struggle for them just to have a meeting. Seems we should close the book on the Failure Club. Save the taxpayers some expense."

Yvonne didn't respond at first, gazing instead into the distance. Her mouth tightened when she opened it to speak.

"You don't have dependents, right?"

"Yeah, just myself."

"Thing is, the man said 'substantial and sufficient contacts.' Substantial. And this is a crisis time. Our work—that is, our *report*—will get more attention than in humdrum times. It's career-building time, DeWitte. I have a little son. I want to have a good report—'stellar,' if possible. I know it's not the same with you. But it seems you should care a *little*, at least."

DeWitte was taken aback. Care about what? The opportunity? Her? Things in general? He didn't want to get into this with her. Anyway, she was the senior agent.

"Of course I care," he said. "If you want to press on, I'm right with you. It's the same hours worked one way or another."

She seemed satisfied. He didn't know how long they'd be partners but, if it couldn't be fun, at least he didn't want hassles. Interpersonal relationships were a pain. Keep things superficial!

They skirted Indianapolis and drove north and east, toward the town of Argentina. The Galactic Retreat Center, customary meeting place for the Failure Club, preceded the town. Reached by a long gravel driveway, it consisted of a barn-like building with a small addition on one end. It had faded white paint and greenish shingles. A garden near the addition was being tended by two young men, while an older man stood and watched. He wore a gold-colored smock, somewhat frayed, above slacks and gym shoes. When he noticed the approaching vehicle, he tossed his beverage can into a pile of garden debris. As the agents walked up, he made a steeple of his hands and smiled. The declining sun raised glints in his thinning silver hair, which was parted in the middle.

"I am Superior Sho," he stated. "These are Brothers Mohar and Kyat. How may we assist you in attaining happiness?"

"Well!" said Yvonne. "This sounds promising!"

The agents identified themselves and asked about the Failure Club. The superior stopped smiling.

"Yes, they rent the facility once or twice a month. I don't like to do it but we need the income. We stay at our place in town when they're here, so I don't know what they do. Just some sort of meetings, I suppose, then some of them camp in the parking field. Again, something I must tolerate. Please the customer, you know. Would you like a tour?"

The interior of the building was mostly one big space, three tatami mats spread in a corner with a couple more rolled up. A small plastic table held a clay teapot and stacked cups. Another corner held piles of folding chairs. Sho led the agents to the addition at one end of the building. The small space inside was enclosed by kitchen equipment and a passage to the outside. They went through to a field scuffed with tire tracks and old campfires. The only vehicle present was an aging pickup truck, the planet Saturn and "G.R.C." painted on its door.

"It's paid for," Sho smirked.

As he led them around the far side of the building, back toward the garden area, DeWitte noticed an apparent outhouse among the trees.

"No indoor plumbing?" he queried.

"Ah, no," Sho responded. "Not for that."

"Mr. Sho," said Yvonne, "does the Failure Club keep any records here? Any computer equipment?"

"No. No records, no computers. We've had a few deliveries for them, supplies for their projects. But those, too, are failures. Those big crates over there have been sitting for months. The equipment inside is already rusty."

He waved toward the three crates. Too big and heavy to

lift, they'd apparently been pushed against the side of the building with a vehicle.

"It was for bottling," said Sho. "Just scrap now, at best."

DeWitte stepped over to inspect the crates. Yvonne and the superior kept walking toward the garden, where Kyat and Mohar were working on opposite ends. Kyat, the closer, was spreading something from a bucket around the bases of plants. A pungent odor emanated from his handiwork.

"Is that—?" Yvonne began.

"Yes," Sho beamed. "Shit from the outhouse! We waste nothing. All is one in the unity of the galaxy!"

She stared at him a moment, then turned and strode away.

"I'll be in the car!" she shouted to DeWitte.

He watched her aggressive walk, the slam of the car door, her digging in her purse. Returning to Sho, he noted Kyat's activity.

"She grossed out?" the superior asked.

"Yeah, I guess so."

"Think I can get one of those cigarettes?"

"I wouldn't ask just now."

Slightly abashed, Sho offered to show DeWitte a banner left behind by the Failure Club. They reentered the building and Sho pulled the rolled-up cloth from behind the stacked folding chairs.

"They left it on the wall, but I didn't want it up there a long time."

Unfurling the banner, DeWitte saw an orange symbol on purple background, the symbol consisting of a *V* resting on a line inside a circle.

"A sign of peace?"

"No," said Sho, "the Phoenix. The goal of the club, I suppose: to rise again from failure. Perhaps false advertising."

DeWitte studied the banner, drawing a blank as to any further meaning. From outside, several blasts of the car horn broke his reverie. He thanked Superior Sho and hastened out to his senior agent.

BEYOND THE FAILURE CLUB

She had him stop for a bottle of rum, which they drank with cola and ice from their motel's vending machines. Yvonne downed her first one quickly. DeWitte was neither a rum nor a cola drinker, but he sensed he should accommodate and so steadily imbibed.

"God," she said, "it's all so ridiculous."

"Yeah, well, not to worry. We'll get our report, all right. We'll just edit it."

"What do you mean?"

"Oh, skip some of the lunacy, make it seem reasonable to keep making contacts."

Yvonne mused a moment.

"And make *those* sound good, too. Without fabricating, of course."

"Of course."

She swirled the pretty liquid in her tumbler. It complemented her pensive face, attractive to DeWitte in the banality of the room. She drank from the tumbler and drained it again of its color.

"Ah! You know, DeWitte, you pleasantly surprise me."

"Hey, you said you wanted a 'stellar' report. Well, I want to be stellar, too! Here's to the stars, partner!"

• • •

The president of the Failure Club, Dr. Xyntius, had again driven to Lansing to meet with Sokki, guiding light of the Talons for Earth Freedom. The Failure Club had been a good enough recruiting pool in the Talons' earlier days, but Sokki had expanded the group with talent from the West and the Southeast. He'd watched their actions with satisfaction from just over the border in Windsor, where he had his landscaping business. Well over six feet tall, he was broad-shouldered but narrow in the hips. He had short whitish hair atop a pale face with watery gray eyes. His stare was disarming.

Dr. Jon Xyntius, a professor of physics, was tall, barrel-chested, and bald. Since Dirtbag's Tavern, where they were meeting, was between a university and government offices, he blended well with the locals. Sokki, on the other hand, would not blend anywhere, so Jon always felt uneasy with him. His companion's deadly role, if exposed, would be the ruin of both of them.

"Had lunch?" Sokki inquired.

"I had a late breakfast."

He ordered a stein of the dark beer Sokki was drinking. They were at a table in an open, half-filled area, daylight slanting in through small windows.

"They interviewed your wife, then?" Sokki probed.

"Yes, straight after talking with Marlena."

"Who?"

"Marlena. Middle-aged realtor, has trouble keeping her license."

"Oh, yeah. Wonder why they talked to *her*?"

"They obviously don't know who the Talons are. The only one they hit so far is Mary Ellen, and that was probably an accident. They saw her at the hospital. The Private thinks they came to the house first but were scared off by his Halloween props."

Sokki chuckled.

"So they put a couple of bozos on us."

"It sure seems that way. When they talked with Lauren, they let her go off on a tangent about her trips to New Mexico, puffing her academic work to disguise her little affair. As if I cared. She apparently thought *I* arranged for them to interview her!"

"Yeah, right. Of course, they got nothing useful about you, your trips and such?"

"No, what could they get? She knows nothing about the Talons, has only contempt for the Failure Club. No, they left as they came: empty-handed."

Sokki nodded distractedly, a sign the subject was changing.

"You've heard about Collins?"

"Yes. Found in the lagoon, south shore area in Chicago. I thought he lived on the north side."

"Well, dopers, you know. They can turn up anywhere."

"Yes. Sad, but he *had* become a problem. No longer useful as a Talon. That and he knew too much."

"I'm thinking," said Sokki, "those two clowns have his name. They might see his death as connected to the club, their investigation."

"Would they even *know* about his death, though?"

"Yeah, no credit to them. The report would've popped up in Home Sec's data bank, copy to the clowns' file on us."

"So who might they go after? Derek?"

"Derek ran with Collins awhile, but he's out of those nitwits' league. He can handle himself okay. I'm a little more concerned about Lyme. As secretary, he's been the club's most active officer, the Web contact and all. He had a lot of contact with Collins, along with other Talons, being our first field boss. All that would be okay, only I don't know that stonewalling is among his talents."

"Yes, Allan tends toward flamboyance. He can be careless at times. No disloyal intent, of course."

"He's a tempting source of info, even for bumblers. I think we should have something in place to pack him off if necessary."

"Have him take a trip somewhere?"

"Yeah."

"He has a wife and children, a house, not to mention his practice as a chiropractor. There are major financial considerations."

"They'll all be covered."

Dr. Xyntius leaned forward.

"I take it, you mean by your deeper contacts."

"The guild, yes. We'll get all we want now through Montreal. They reward performance."

"It'll still be tricky. Andrew will have to fill his shoes with the Talons."

"Full confidence. Andrew's been great on the projects."

"Then there's the Failure Club. Without Allan, it'll hardly have a structure. It could fall apart."

Sokki looked off into the rays of sunlight slanting through small windows.

"Screw the club," he said. "It's just an old shell that we're shedding."

• • •

Having completed two consecutive interviews with respected professionals, agents Gormer and Billups were feeling upbeat as they entered Illinois. They had their pick of Failure Club members in the south suburbs but, feeling more polished now, decided to avoid the less savory. They thus bypassed Lar Cody, director of a federal facility until indicted on child porn charges.

"There's gotta be a huge federal file already," said DeWitte. "We can claim redundance."

"I'm cool with that," Yvonne responded. "Maybe we can say the same about Arch here. Convicted of cruelty to animals for ritual sacrifices in a cult he ran."

"Ugh! That'd be local jurisdiction, but what the heck. We can stretch the notion. Anyhow, what terrorist bunch would trust an idiot like that?"

"True, true. You're coming right along, DeWitte."

They decided to interview Janus Smyth and his common-law wife, Kitty Eccles, who had no major charges. On arriving at their bungalow, however, the agents found it was the weediest property on the block. When Janus answered the door, he was in a similar state—disheveled, haggard, and unshaven. Kitty was passed out on a couch, a melted scotch-on-rocks on the coffee table before her.

"Is this about UFOs?" Janus asked.

"We'll check back later," said Yvonne.

Returning to the car, DeWitte gave her an amused look.

"Officially not home?"

"No, we ID'd ourselves. Put them down as drunk and uncommunicative. It's their own damn fault, plus we get credit for a contact."

Now ahead of schedule, they decided to see Derek Russell earlier than planned. His karate school was in the inner city, in an area that grew more hazardous as the day progressed. It was still peaceful when the agents arrived, the stagnant neighborhood uninspired by the crisp spring sunshine. Derek was chatting with a couple of teenagers in the undersized instruction area. His eyes were intense beneath his short Afro, and he had a strong, lithe physique. The teens drifted away when the agents identified themselves.

"It's strictly defensive," Derek said, "all we teach here. We don't train anyone for tournaments and that. We do the philosophy behind it, human values and all, try to tie it in with other programs in the community."

Yvonne nodded approvingly.

"Did Norman Collins used to come here?"

Derek hesitated a moment, but otherwise didn't react.

"Collins from the club? The Failure Club? Stopped by once or twice but he wasn't involved in the program. He wasn't, you know, ready for the discipline. I saw that he passed recently. That what you're investigating?"

"Partly," Yvonne replied.

"According to the phone logs," said DeWitte, "you and Collins used to have a lot of contact. Was that Failure Club business?"

"No, not really. We shared a ride to meetings, but most of the calling was personal stuff. He was a screwed-up guy. You prob'ly know that. I thought I could help the dude, like I help people here in the community."

"The calling fell off in the months before his death."

"Yeah, he was going downhill. Into some bad shit, I guess. People I didn't know. I couldn't help him any more, he wouldn't listen."

"Derek," said Yvonne, "do you travel very often?"

"Travel? No, they keep me pretty busy here. Once in a while professionally, check out karate in other areas. I was out Denver way on that. Maybe you saw a record somewhere."

"You don't use the travel discounts from the Failure Club?"

"Hey, I'd like to. But like I say, I'm heavy into the community just now. It pretty much takes all my time."

"Except for Failure Club meetings," said DeWitte.

"Well, yeah."

"If I may ask," said Yvonne, "why did you join a club with that name? So—I don't know, downbeat?"

Derek smiled, looked away toward the street.

"I had this book, you know. Self-published, about karate, my thoughts and all. It was written for the inner city. Guess I was kind of naïve thinking it'd sell, make some money for the center here. So I saw this Failure Club and thought I'd look for some ideas on coming back, some inspiration. It's what I see as 'constructive humility.'"

After a pause, Yvonne offered Derek her hand.

"You're a credit to the community and society. Keep up the good work."

After they'd left, Derek crossed the street to a small grocery store and used a pay phone inside.

"Andrew? Yeah. Those lackeys came by. Nah, it was so easy I thought they were putting me on. But they got nothing, man. Zippo."

• • •

After lunch, Yvonne and DeWitte considered seeing Max Tonger, a former restaurant owner who'd been bilked by his partner. The agents wanted one more contact before their grand finale, a talk with a second Failure Club officer.

"I don't know," said Yvonne, "his status as a failure seems pretty obvious. Our report might be better if we went after this

Charybdis—Henrietta Dawes, really—who's got a dispute with her employer. Big girl, three hundred some, suing for accommodation."

DeWitte drove to the north side social service agency where Charybdis/Henrietta was employed. They found, however, that she wasn't at work, having called in sick for the day.

"It's one of the issues in her grievance," a supervisor explained. "We got her the heavy-duty chair, but she also wants extra sick leave to rest from work."

The agents returned to their car.

"Want to reconsider Mr. Tonger?" asked DeWitte.

"No," Yvonne replied. "Less is more on that one."

"Kinda early to knock off for the day."

"I agree."

"What, then? The other officer?"

Yvonne gave a coy smile.

"We'd have a wrap, partner! Plus a free night in this toddlin' town!"

DeWitte laughed.

"Yvonne, like you said about me, 'you're coming right along.'"

They had their choice of either Dr. Lyme, the secretary, or Mr. Singh, the treasurer. Dr. Lyme's clinic was out in the northwest suburbs, beyond the airport, while Mr. Singh's accounting firm was downtown, a much shorter drive from where they were.

"We can get to our party sooner if we go with the treasurer," DeWitte noted.

"And we'd be close to the best spots," added Yvonne.

"Say no more."

He pulled away with a squeal of tires and they headed for "the Loop." Arriving downtown, they left the car in a parking garage and walked to the large building that housed Singh's firm. An elevator brought them to the company's floor. They searched the names on a wall directory but, to their surprise, did not find a C.R. Singh.

"Yes, he works here," confirmed the receptionist, "but are you sure he's the one you're supposed to see?"

"No doubt about it," DeWitte assured her.

They were directed to the rear of the floor, toward a corner, with a sign on the way that read *Library*. It was actually more of a mail room, though there were shelves of books and periodicals along one wall. Mr. Singh was running envelopes through a postage meter. He was a study in concentration with wavy black hair and horn-rimmed glasses. He'd loosened his tie in the stuffy room and rolled up his sleeves. He was startled by the agents' appearance, but quickly composed himself.

"This is just temporary," he explained, gesturing about the room. "In six or seven weeks I'll again be a junior associate. Of course, this work is also of value to the firm. Combination librarian and mail clerk. I'm upbeat. I'm not stultified. But this is not my true status. There were snafus. They wanted to show concern—please the client, you know?"

"We understand," said Yvonne. "But as treasurer of the Failure Club, you are also its only accountant?"

"Yes!" he beamed. "I handle all financial records and insure accuracy. Of course, the other officers have access."

"But you're the one in charge, with the authority."

"Yes," Singh smiled, "I have the authority."

"Are you aware," DeWitte injected, "that the IRS is auditing your tax returns?"

"Oh, that!" A wave at the air. "Simple misunderstandings. We support charities, worthy causes, and we offer group discount programs. Sometimes they are combined. Over a whole year, it becomes very complicated what is going to charity, what for expenses, what for our pleasure, et cetera, et cetera."

"Yes, well, they're also concerned with large electronic transfers to the club expense account, which dissolve soon after deposit."

Mr. Singh raised his eyebrows, went palms-upward with

his hands.

"I've been told the club has outside contributors, and our members of course travel on our projects."

"Like the one with the bottling equipment?" asked Yvonne.

Mr. Singh giggled.

"Please, that was so silly. To sell water for profit, but we had no well, no spring or anything!"

He giggled again, but then the shelves of books caught his eye. He quickly sobered.

"There have always been accountants in our family," he said, "all the way back to the dawn of corporations. My brothers and cousins, our parents, generations before. The Failure Club was a lifesaver for me, it restored my dignity—my belief in God, perhaps. I'm sorry. I don't mean to be too personal, but—"

He looked down at his hands, which moved restlessly against each other.

"That's okay," Yvonne soothed, "let it all hang out."

"I owe a lot to the club, so I'm happy to serve it. I know the members are failures, like me—as I was, I mean—but I'm happy to serve them. We help each other, you know, to rise again in dignity."

DeWitte was reminded of the banner that Superior Sho had shown him, the symbol of the Phoenix.

"I think we've come full circle," he told Yvonne, "like we have the full scoop on the Failure Club. Maybe we can move on to—well, our other pressing matters."

Yvonne suppressed a smile.

"Yes, Agent Gormer, I agree. Thank you for your cooperation, Mr. Singh."

The treasurer sat for a while after they'd left, distracted from the mail he'd been processing. Sounds of work activity floated in from the greater office. Mr. Singh felt uncomfortable. A new disruption had been heaped on the one he was struggling to resolve here at the firm. Working the postage meter and moving paper around would not remove this new anxiety. He needed help again, he saw. There was a phone in the mail room. There would be no shame in calling Dr. Xyntius, explaining it all to him. He was president of the club and should know anyway. And maybe he could help, renew one's strength to rise again.

Dr. Xyntius listened patiently, waiting until Mr. Singh had no more to add. He than assured the treasurer that he'd handled the situation perfectly.

"You were appropriately candid. The club has nothing to hide. All of our dealings are legitimate and with the noblest intentions for our members and society."

"Thank you, sir. It's just that I was so surprised. I look up from my work and—boom!—there's Homeland Security. Asking about our simple club, of all things. I had no chance to prepare for them, to have the demeanor—"

"Now, now. Don't worry about it. It's over and you did fine. In fact, it might be fortunate that this happened because it justifies my confidence in you. You see, Mr. Singh, I want to give you a greater role in the club, one with prestige that I think you deserve, and can *handle*."

"A new role?"

"Yes. Dr. Lyme will be moving to Sweden for a while—indefinitely—so I'll need you to run the Failure Club meetings in my absence. You'll also assume his status as main contact for the members and the public. All of this, of course, may be listed on your professional résumé as leadership credentials. And don't worry, I'll appoint a sergeant-at-arms to help keep order at those meetings."

Mr. Singh absorbed the news, groped for a response.

"Well, thank you, sir. I'll do my best."

It seemed so banal as it left his mouth, yet Dr. Xyntius laughed in satisfaction.

"I know you will, Mr. Singh, as always. And it'll be more than enough to accomplish our goals. You'll play a vital part in changing many people's lives."

CHAPTER 9

Andrew had to smile as he walked the quiet street, his mind picturing Puck springing from the hedges. His wife had rented the video of *A Midsummer Night's Dream*, thinking it would go nicely that night while their daughter was sleeping. That would be after this meeting in the park with Sokki, someone as strange to him as Puck would have been. Sokki was from Windsor, in Canada, and guided the actions of the Talons for Earth Freedom, of which Andrew was a rising member. Sokki's identity, however, was unknown to most of the Talons. Andrew had learned it just that day from Dr. Xyntius, president of the Failure Club, the shell group from which Talons had been recruited. Sokki, the president said, was coming to Andrew's neighborhood on the outskirts of Madison, Wisconsin. He'd be in the park this summer evening, where he and Andrew could talk as if they were strollers meeting.

Andrew, with his clean-cut good looks, worked as a counselor in the local school system. His wife, Corinne, had been a teacher until the birth of their daughter the previous year. Corinne knew about the Failure Club and accepted it as connected to Andrew's work. She did *not* know of his involvement with the Talons for Earth Freedom, and would have been shocked to learn of it. Her husband was educated and non-violent, while the Talons employed brutal force in their campaign against corporate power. Andrew could not reveal his secret role to Corinne because his purpose was to protect her and Orchid, their daughter, from both the corruption in society and the consequences of his actions. He'd committed his life to the Talons' success, but those close to him mustn't suffer for it. Thus were set the limits of what he would risk: for himself, death; for his family, nothing.

Walking now through the orange-tinted evening sunlight, Andrew was reminded again of the "indexes of quality" that he and Corinne discussed. Their life together and with Orchid, his job, their network of family and friends, their health and tastes, all amounted to what should be a fulfilling lifestyle for them. Corinne, in fact, seemed happy and satisfied. But as Andrew looked around, past Madison and the mainstream media, he saw that their social and financial network was in fact quite thin, and that beyond it lay chaos.

Though he was paid fairly for his work, Andrew was aware of others in society who received much more for less effort, less learning, less caring about their fellow man. He'd always known, of course, about the rich, but unlike his father he didn't accept them. He'd read Auchincloss novels, then noted the tenacity of "old money," as well as the legacies of ruthless "entrepreneurs" and their offspring. High-placed bankers and corporate officers, financiers, and others formed a society within the society, one that stretched its tentacles internationally. Their politicians presented stubborn wrongness as strength; rational compromise as weakness. A crude appeal to nationalism would thus be used to justify a war, all the time serving the corporate and related agendas. The public could be distracted with stock issues such as abortion and gun control, or lulled to sleep through corporate control of media and culture. It left a population that was poorly informed, its intellects declining from disuse, its values grotesque.

Even among family and friends, Andrew found a dimming awareness of the corporate designs on health care, social security, and the environment. Beyond his fragile circle lay the confused mass of society, with its endless ghettos, violence, and self-abasement. The two-party system, America's model for the world, had been co-opted by corporate power. Fringe groups on the left and right provided impotent opposition, serving only to legitimize the existing monopoly. No, beyond a few friends and his modest income, there was no supportive network for Andrew's family. This was what he saw and resented, what he chose to fight against in the Talons for Earth Freedom.

He came to the park. There was no one in sight except two small children with their mother, by the swings on the far side. He sat on a bench and waited.

The video would be good later, Andrew thought. They didn't sit together by the television as much as they used to. The news was shallow and repetitive, the entertainment stupid. The scenes from the classic comedy would blend nicely with the loud whirr of crickets through their open window. He loved Corinne, had to make the most of even the simplest moments with her. Perhaps especially those.

"The new chiropractor, I presume?"

Andrew turned to the voice, which came from a clump of small trees behind the bench. He at first didn't see anyone, but then sensed the speaker had moved behind him, to the other end of the bench. Sokki's tread was soft and swift.

"Chiropractor?"

"Dr. Lyme's replacement."

The tall man with whitish hair sat and crossed his legs, gazed through the dying sunlight at the people by the swings. He might be very pale, Andrew thought, though it was hard to tell in the orange light.

"I appreciate the confidence, but aren't I just a stand-in?"

"We'll see," said Sokki. "Things are in flux."

Andrew had recently been made field supervisor of the Midwest segment of the Talons, supplanting Dr. Lyme, who was now in Sweden. The move had followed widespread investigations by the Department of Homeland Security. Dr. Xyntius and Sokki had seen Dr. Lyme as too visible and risky as a target of investigation.

"I thought it was time we met," said Sokki. "Things are changing with the Talons. We're cutting loose from the Failure Club, for one."

"Will Dr. Xyntius still be president?"

"For a while, till he can dump it. He hasn't been that busy with the Talons, anyway. He's just been carrying orders from me. But he won't be going the way of Dr. Lyme. We'll eventually need a political wing in addition to field ops, which then becomes the military wing. Dr. X is a natural for the job."

"Yes, he was a third-party candidate and all."

"Exactly. Also for now, he stays official head of the three Talon groups—yours, the West, and the Southeast. The western people don't know me yet, but we'll be fixing that and Dr. X can start easing out."

"So I'll be working with you more than him?"

Sokki gave him his stare, which was disarming, but added a smile.

"Any problem with that?"

"No, sir."

"Okay. But lose the 'sir.' I only go by the one name."

"Okay, Sokki."

The Canadian hesitated, turning his gaze to the trees and the street, where lights had come on. He might have been waiting for a reaction, Andrew thought, but he had nothing to say. He was there to receive orders.

"I'll be around a few days," Sokki said. "Don't worry, I won't show up at your house. But stay with the news. There's something going down with our Southeast friends."

"A project?"

"Right. That's the other reason I'm here with you. In case we need to follow it up somehow, mobilize in the Midwest, I'm here to work with you."

"Is it likely?"

"No. But we cover every angle now. Any and all carelessness departed with Dr. Lyme."

"Good."

"Don't get me wrong. He was dedicated and plenty smart—still is—but we don't need all that panache. We need invisibility—quiet, effective force. Of course, we claim responsibility to maximize the effect."

"By the way, we're having houseguests this weekend. One of the Talons—Bar, along with his girlfriend. Should I not tell him that you're around?"

"Right. I'll stay incognito with the operatives for now. They know they have support; that's enough. If I call your house, I'll be 'Mr. Peters.'"

"Okay. And I'll watch the news."

Sokki looked away into the distance.

"They're a frisky group down there. Members have felt more confined, restricted by the culture than here and in the West. They're itching to knock it on its ear. My main concern is that they might get carried away."

"I'll be standing by."

Sokki smiled and made a move to clap him on the shoulder. He stopped short, however.

"Whoops! That'd mean you had contact with me."

Andrew waited respectfully. A light comment from such a powerful man, he thought, had no proper response.

"Your family's waiting for you," said Sokki. "I'll be in contact."

He was rising from the bench while still speaking. Quickly, quietly, he was back in the trees from which he'd emerged. Andrew watched the spot where Sokki had disappeared, sensing a spirit of hope in the new summer night. We're going to win, he thought.

He walked home to the rising whirr of crickets. It was crude and aggressive as it claimed the gathering night, yet something in him responded to it.

• • •

Little Orchid was playing in her splash pool, dappled by the languid summer sun filtering through overhanging boughs. Nearby, Corinne was showing Ulitreé their ample garden, receiving advice on organic food production. Ulitreé was a sales clerk at Primal Dream, which specialized in health products and New Age solutions in Flag City, Indiana. She was visiting with her lover, Byron Invictus, usually called Bar, who watched from the shaded patio with Andrew. Corinne listened earnestly within the short, dark sweep of her hair, while blond and braided Ulitreé imparted her wisdom.

"She was a nudist once," Bar informed Andrew.

"Ah. Well, the pool's a little small for her."

Bar looked at Andrew sidelong, then they shared a chuckle. The remains of lunch were on the table between them. Bar was somewhat older than Andrew, side streaks of gray in his dark blond hair. He was the night case manager at a rural mental health clinic.

"We can look at the school now," Andrew said. "Any activities will be over for the day."

"Sure. What'd they have today—vacation Bible school?"

"No, sports camps and such. VBS got the boot on a lawsuit. Church and state, et cetera."

"Hey, progress is being made."

"It can always swing back again. Especially now."

"You can say *that* again!"

Bar was a natural for cynicism, Andrew thought, but he wasn't given to detailed discussions. This may have been due to his settling for a B.A., whereas Andrew had gone for a master's degree. Mental appetites are honed by higher education, as is the brain by satisfying them. Though they worked in the same general field, therefore, they could only confer on an equal basis for so long. Within the Talons for Earth Freedom, Andrew had been told that Bar would remain an operative, while he himself would ascend the leadership ladder. He accepted this, but he also wanted Bar as a friend. And by inviting him and Ulitreé for the weekend, he furtively allowed his family a taste of his Talons experience.

"We're heading over to the school," he told Corinne.

"We'll be at one of the health food stores. Ulitreé's going to show me what's good."

"Uh-oh. Is there exotic cooking in my future?"

"Let's say 'experimental.'"

"Well, just don't get carried away."

"Why not?" Ulitreé spoke up. "That's the fun of it!"

Andrew was enjoying this interlude with Bar and Ulitreé, his conversation with Sokki seeming like a bizarre dream. At the same time, he was aware of boundaries on his relaxation, beyond which every action and thought must consider the Talons. He was therefore quiet on the ride to the school, thinking but not speaking of Sokki's information.

"That was a great dinner last night," said Bar. "Long time since we had one with other people. I mean nice like that."

"We'll be doing it again tonight. Hope you don't mind classical music. It's a Saturday thing with Corinne."

"That'll be a break for me. Ulitreé goes for those long, meditative numbers. Music to moon by, I think of it. Don't tell her, though."

"Keep a secret from a friend?"

"That's how people *stay* friends."

They pulled into the near-empty lot and Andrew used his passkey to enter the school. He showed Bar the gym, where they shot a few flat-footed hoops, and the cafeteria, devoid of food smells in the idle summertime. They spent some time in the computer lab, and the other labs, before coming to Andrew's office and the conference rooms. There was a second desk in Andrew's room, cleared for the summer except for an artificial flower in a painted clay vase. His own desk was semi-cluttered, various forms and correspondence sorted into low stacks. He flipped through them while Bar tried the seats in the conference rooms.

"Hey now, these are ass-savers!" Bar called out. "You're one-up already on Five-County Rehab!"

Glancing through the forms, Andrew was reminded that he'd left some unfinished, wanting to give his entries more thought. The messages and articles were also items that he'd left for later. When Bar came in from the conference room, Andrew suggested he check out the faculty lounge. He himself would follow shortly, after this inventory.

The papers felt insubstantial in Andrew's hands. The banality of the school procedures, the formal courtesy of the messages, the abstractness of the articles—it was all a vaporous blur. The quiet of the empty school made these forms diaphanous, spider webs of hindrance to be brushed aside. They weren't like this during the school year, of course. The issues then were solid, priorities he arranged to leave time for his work with the Talons. Now, however, he felt awkward in this chair, the power of the Talons looming over him. They were a force for immediate, concrete social action, before which banality and abstractions paled. His job, Andrew saw, was now only for the wages. He used them to finance his life with Corinne and Orchid. Aside from that, his commitment was elsewhere.

Bar was returning from the lounge.

"Andrew, there's something you better see."

He followed his friend to the sunny, couch-lined room and saw that the television was on. Bar had it tuned to an all-news station, where a reporter was talking over scenes of people on stretchers, then a building and its interior. Police types were poking around, those inside wearing gas masks.

"The substance has been identified as CS-type tear gas," said the reporter, "concentration about military level. It was delivered in bogus beverage tanks, using delayed timing devices. The tanks were left at two points in the hall sometime after the president's departure, when security was eased."

"Where is this?" Andrew asked Bar.

"Florida, a political fund-raiser."

"Any deaths?"

"One, a heart attack. Sixty-some others hospitalized, at least one critical."

Andrew watched the screen, which switched to some spokesman reading a statement of outrage. As this went on, a running text at the bottom of the screen informed that the Talons for Earth Freedom had claimed responsibility. In Andrew's mind, this message was spoken in Sokki's voice, the man reading the statement drowned out for a moment. Andrew watched calmly, unsurprised, as the station cut back to the anchor desk, then to a hospital where victims of the attack were being treated.

"Think it's really our southern group?" asked Bar. "Not copycats?"

"Yeah, I'd say it's us. Timing's about right since the last project."

"Aiming kinda high this time. The president—"

"Uh-huh. I'm surprised. It's quite a step."

"I guess we can expect repercussions."

Andrew shrugged.

"We've been living with them already. That dragnet after the last actions, investigation of the Failure Club—"

He shot Bar a smile with half-closed eyes. Two agents from Homeland Security had come up dry, given the club a clean bill of health in the crackdown on suspicious organizations. Most of the members interviewed were oblivious to the presence of Talons within the club.

"Think they'll come after us again?"

"No, the report from last time is a protection now. Anyhow, we're phasing the club out as a cover."

"Yeah? We don't need it?"

"It was a recruiting pool. Now the Talons are expanded by

absorbing other groups. Our western folks have been coverless since they joined us."

"And our southern friends?"

"Their philosophy discussions nosedived. Just some folks they don't trust still doing the wine and cheese."

Bar laughed.

"So we're becoming phantoms? Exist only in our actions, then disappear? No connections?"

"I guess you could say that. For now, anyway. With time—and success—we might need representatives to deal with the government, negotiate. Participate in the power structure."

"No kidding? Like a political party?"

"Yeah, maybe. I'm just theorizing, of course."

Bar gave a knowing nod.

"Uh-huh. Just theorizing."

He let it go at that. Andrew admired Bar's discretion, especially since Bar was the older between them. It was probably one reason for their truncated discussions. Bar knew his limitations, wouldn't stray out of his depth. He was content to remain an operative and was a good one. He watched the screen now as news of the attack repeated, Andrew also watching but from another perspective. What about the human element here? Shouldn't they be concerned about the suffering they'd caused, the one or two deaths? He knew the answer his higher-ups would give, which Bar accepted without question: the real cause of the suffering was the evil the Talons were fighting—in which, actually, most of these victims were participating. Andrew let it pass provisionally, since without the Talons he had no movement. But in his heart he would never accept killing, or reckless assault, as a means to an end. It moved him too close in spirit to the generals and politicians who labored for the corporate powers he despised.

• • •

Sunday passed quietly. Corinne and Ulitreé took Orchid to

the zoo, with a side tour of the local university campus. Andrew and Bar watched baseball on television, a way to wait for more news on the previous day's attack. For Andrew, it was also a way to be near the phone in case Sokki called. The long day slipped by, however, with no word from the Talons' mentor. Finally, as they were finishing supper, Corinne informed Andrew that a Mr. Peters was on the line for him.

"The train station," Sokki said, "tomorrow morning at eleven. Two strangers on a bench again."

"Okay," Andrew replied, then lowered his voice. "What about Bar? They're expecting to leave after breakfast."

"Let'em go. Just you and me for now."

"Right."

When Corinne asked who Mr. Peters was, Andrew said he was a salesman. This satisfied her, as always, because of the limitless trust between them. Andrew had no qualms about hiding his Talons work from her, because he intended no malice. The work was for her sake and Orchid's, and it was better for them not to know of it. As he took Corinne in his arms that night, as they made love, Andrew felt confident he was doing his best for them. He therefore deserved these moments with this beautiful dark-haired woman, kissing her frank, balanced features, viewing and stroking her strong, sculpt body. Nonetheless, he felt lucky. Away from the risks of life, amid the sounds of summer night, Andrew wondered if others had it this good. What, he thought absurdly, did Sokki do for sex? He laughed softly and continued his probes, watching Corinne's shoulder squirm, her breast shift below. From far off, a train whistle sounded, then briefly repeated.

"Do you like Ulitreé?" she'd asked.

"I think she's good for Bar."

A kiss, then "Yes, she's nice."

"Only what?"

"I don't know," said Corinne, "there's something about her opinions. Kind of stilted, clinical."

"She was a nudist once."

"Once?"

"She quit as she got older, when her body changed. Bar told me. She wouldn't have sex for a while, either."

"Hm, I guess that ties in. She's into strong statements on things, dogmas. But she'll disown them for her convenience. Then other things become dogmas."

"A chain of beliefs. People can go through life that way."

"I guess it's better than *no* beliefs."

"Yes, I suppose it is."

Except, Andrew might have added, for those controlling our society and seeking to control the world. Without an aggressive ideology, or confidence in wealth and their right to it, they would not be the smothering force that they are. There were even signs they saw divine approval of their agenda, encouraged in this by accommodating preachers. For people without power, of course, it was better to believe in *anything* rather than nothing. Andrew still accompanied Corinne to church when she wanted to go. But what he saw as best was the healthy skepticism, perhaps cynicism, that he was able to express and act on with the Talons. It put them in direct opposition to the destructive mentality of corporate oppression. With more empowerment, they would defeat the belief in empire, or at least mitigate its effects.

Bar and Ulitreé departed early Monday morning. Andrew helped straighten the room they'd used and then told Corinne he had errands downtown. He arrived there early for his appointment with Sokki, so he browsed in bookstores until eleven o'clock. Proceeding to the train station, he again saw no sign of his colleague, who he thought should stand out. He sat on a well-worn bench among scattered fellow waiters. Almost at once, a tall form moved smoothly around a corner. The man had a straw hat with ample brim, hiding his features, but the quick, quiet strides announced it was Sokki. He joined Andrew on the waiting bench.

"Get the houseguests off okay?"

"Yeah, early on. Bar was scheduled to work tonight."

Sokki nodded, sweeping the station with his gaze, the hat brim masking his potent stare.

"Good, good. Yeah, we'll sit tight for now, let'em think the attack was on the president."

"Isn't that what it was?"

"Hell, no. The near-miss angle works, shakes people up a bit, but it was aimed right along at the supporters. You show up at these things, you chip in your funds, you're a target. The president's just a figurehead, after all. It's the people behind him that're the prime enemy."

"These weren't the biggest players, though."

"Yeah, but they'll get the message. And if it *had* been those Permindex types, we'd have used more than tear gas. They know it, too."

"Well, the SAM must have gotten their attention."

The previous winter, the Talons had used a surface-to-air missile to down a helicopter. The chopper had contained the leading conservative news spinner on television.

"And we might be expanding our arsenal," Sokki said.

Andrew frowned, momentarily puzzled. They already had access to most guns and explosives.

"You don't mean—beyond conventional?"

A wide, thin-lipped smile appeared beneath the hat brim.

"I'll be pressing for it with our backers. A mini-nuke. After this last action, they can see we wouldn't waste it. We simply wait for the right occasion, the core enemies—"

"There's one available?"

"There might be. One or more."

Andrew was silent, pondering the thought of participating in a nuclear attack. Sokki observed him.

"I don't think this lowers us to their level. *They're* the merchants of death, after all. We're simply their executioners. The mini would be from their own facility, their own planning."

Andrew nodded, not quite able to claim "poetic justice."

"There's irony in this for both of us," Sokki continued.

"For most of the Talons, in fact. We're against the wars, along with other corporate oppression, yet we use violence to oppose it. I first moved to Canada to avoid the draft for Vietnam, didn't move back after the general pardon. I've watched things closely, though. I see the same crap that disrupted my life continuing into this new century: control by an economic elite of government, society, and culture. It extends internationally, British and others involved, but we've got enough to deal with in North America. Anyway, you cut out the cancer here and you've got the biggest part. The rest will shrivel up. It's not that we *want* to kill, or use violence at all, but after forty years what else is left?"

Andrew hesitated, suddenly feeling better.

"I like the cancer analogy," he said. "I don't know that it's medically accurate, though."

"So clean it up for when you use it yourself. You're the future, Andrew—the most solid younger talent in the Talons for Earth Freedom."

Sokki looked around the room again, feigning idleness. Reaching into a pocket, he brought out a key with an address tag attached. He handed it to Andrew.

"My place in Windsor, command central. Anything happens to me, take what you can use and destroy the rest. Someone from the guild will contact you, but try to get there ahead of them."

"The guild?"

"Our backers, or the hub of our backers—an international network. Maybe there are other hubs. This one's out of Montreal. We've been joined with something much bigger than our own operations. The trick is to maintain autonomy."

Andrew looked at the key.

"Why don't you give this to Dr. Xyntius?"

"He's too visible. Professor of physics with a stormy marriage, third-party candidate, founder of the Failure Club. There's a chance he'd be noticed. It's all just a safeguard, but that's where our strength lies, Andrew. Cover every detail.

It's the way we offset disadvantages—in number, resources, et cetera. We turn less into more by giving them nothing to attack. By being invisible."

Sokki exited in the direction from which he'd come. With the hat and with growing distance, he became just another person walking the street. There's a fine line, Andrew thought, between an extraordinary person and one who just doesn't fit in. Sokki was a winner, and the key to his victory lay in Andrew's pocket.

It was lunchtime, he realized. There were nice restaurants nearby and he had a taste for steak. It would balance the weekend's vegetarianism, their accommodation of Ulitreé.

It would acquaint him again with the taste of blood.

CHAPTER 10

The first month of the academic year had passed at Horizon State, the campus foliage assuming its recruiting-brochure colors. Dr. Xyntius, associate professor of physics, was looking forward to a weekend with his mistress, Miss Diaz, who was also a department secretary. The professor's wife, Lauren, would be at an out-of-state professional conference. Since the visit from Homeland Security regarding her husband's activities, Lauren had herself been more cautious in love affairs. She'd forsworn a summer position at a distant institution and stayed in Michigan, settling for occasional trips to conferences. The coming weekend was an extension of her summer adjustment, and her husband planned to take advantage of it. The summer had been limited, after all, for him and Hilda, so they had a few magical moments coming.

"I'll take you to the apple festival," he said, "at Fenn River Falls. There's a cozy hotel nearby–Jacuzzi, et cetera."

She peered up through round-rimmed glasses.

"Will we get to dine alfresco?"

Xyntius laughed.

BEYOND THE FAILURE CLUB

"Alfresco, alfredo, you name it. Whatever you want, my sweet."

He felt warmed by her smile. She was small, some would say mousey. Since he himself was bearish, people found them an odd couple. It added to the excitement for him, an erotic incongruity he'd explain using the principles of physics: Hilda was the moon attracted to his planetary mass.

"But isn't it early to celebrate apple harvest? Some of the types are still ripening."

He touched her tawny hair, which was nicely styled.

"Details, details. Your specialty, I know. Don't worry, Miss Diaz. There's enough ripe ones for a fest."

She poked his belly.

"And ripe eaters, too."

He'd have picked her up then if they weren't in the office, looked for the nearest soft spot to undress her. As it was, he had to file his impulse away, leave it for an arranged time and place. A year had passed since he'd offered to leave Lauren and make Hilda the new Mrs. Xyntius. But the secretary, with her charming attention to detail, had explained the delicate balance of their relationship and the risk in disrupting it. Xyntius was grateful to her, especially when he considered possible attention to the Failure Club and discovery of the secret group within it. Now, as the Talons for Earth Freedom outgrew their old shell, Hilda could assist in freeing Jon Xyntius from the discarded cover. It would certainly enhance their relationship, but was a subject he must broach with care. Hilda had mixed feelings toward the club. The intimacy of a nice hotel room, in the midst of a romantic getaway, might prove the ideal setting for involving her.

Arriving at the fest, they browsed through stalls of crafts amid sunlit autumn foliage. Amateur efforts in leather and wood reflected various levels of skill, together with wreaths, art, and needlework. Xyntius was tempted to buy a painting or two, but he decided to keep his hands free in case Hilda wanted something. They watched apples being ground in an old cidermaker and tasted some of the end-product. There was honey complete with bees, fresh vegetables and flower bulbs, and a selection of Michigan wines. On Hilda's suggestion, Xyntius bought a bottle for their dinner that night.

"It might not be as good as our usual," he cautioned.

"But it's part of the festival," she smiled.

He was thus carrying a wine bottle as they passed the stage where a band was playing a lively number. Hilda joined in the overhead clapping while Xyntius reflected on how removed he was from militant social action. As long as he kept his priorities straight, he thought, these little flings were okay. They eventually moved on among mimes and the announcement of a log-rolling contest. All the silly trappings, Xyntius thought, but what mattered was that Hilda was happy. They came to the kiddie rides and she glanced around expectantly.

"They don't have the little ponies."

"People thought it was inhumane, having them walk all day in a circle like that. So they're banned."

"I wonder what happened to them?"

"I don't know."

He supposed they'd been moved to another, less sensitive part of the country, though he wouldn't bother Hilda with the thought. It was based on his belief that any corruption or perversion could find a place in American society, because there was no genuine, unifying concept of quality in social standards. A scientific approach was needed, though most people weren't ready for it. They'd only accept it when they saw nothing else was working.

They came to a food tent.

"Looks like it's corn dogs or bratwurst," Hilda observed.

"The brats are more carcinogenic."

"I'll settle for an ice cream."

"Wise choice. We'll dine in style this evening. The restaurant has a deck overlooking the falls."

"Mm, I can hardly wait, My President."

BEYOND THE FAILURE CLUB

He shot her a surprised glance. She'd used the bedroom name quite early. But then, they were far away from the university. Discretion was not a priority. She took his arm as they walked the nature trails, deciding to forgo the attractions at the town stores. Now and then a leaf would fall near them, Hilda observing each one closely. She's entirely into the moment, Xyntius thought, and he almost envied her. But he also valued politics, or couldn't escape it in any case, so he was essentially playing a role in this idyllic setting. It continued into dinner later, and when they made love in the hotel room, where for Hilda he was president of their love nest. She scrambled over him with greater passion this night, so that Xyntius himself was absorbed in the moment, yielding control to the child-sized woman above him. She guided him to a new summit, hovered, then folded forward for detumescence.

"I have plans," he said at breakfast. "They involve you, if you're willing."

She eyed him warily, perhaps fearing another marriage proposal. He had to put her at ease.

"Part of them is *your* plan, really. You wanted me to run for president again. Well, eventually that will happen. If things go right, I mean."

Hilda brightened, her weekend offering yet another treat.

"How?" she asked.

Xyntius returned her smile, but also looked thoughtfully into the middle distance.

"To get back into politics, I'll have to take some time from what I'm doing now. My duties at the university are set in stone, so the place to cut down is the Failure Club. Trouble is, Dr. Lyme–who filled in for me in the past–is off in Sweden indefinitely. Mr. Singh, the treasurer, is having problems with the role, so I need to appoint a replacement for Allan–someone I can trust. Allan was the secretary, of course–ran the meetings, managed the website, the correspondence. You wouldn't have to do as much, of course. Mr. Singh can still help with the meetings–"

"You want me as secretary, Jon? Of the Failure Club?"

"It would be a great help, Hilda. It'd open the window of opportunity for me to return to politics. And it'd only be temporary, of course, until the next election of officers."

Hilda hesitated.

"I don't know what to say. To be secretary of a club, it's not the same as secretary of a department. And the idea of the club, the failure part. I don't agree with it. You know I thought it should be a *Success* Club, not a Failure Club."

"That's what I'm trying to do now, move on to success. But don't be put off by the name. The members don't *want* to fail. They meet to support each other as they work to succeed– *rise up* from failure. The name is just to attract people who have the problem, like a cancer group, family stress group, et cetera."

Hilda was thoughtful, but finally smiled slightly.

"Would it really help you?"

"Absolutely! And I'll be right behind you to help with any problems."

The smile widened.

"Then I'm honored, My President."

With an aggressive wave of his arm, Dr. Xyntius hailed a waitress to demand champagne for the occasion.

• • •

In a Toronto neighborhood bordering on seedy, Sokki and Alypia sat in their hotel room. The building was a converted Victorian mansion with fireplaces in some rooms, including this one. Sokki stared into the logs, unlit though it was dusk and growing chill, while he and Alypia waited for a colleague. He was Anton from the guild, who was making a phone call from his own, simpler room elsewhere in the mansion. He was conferring with colleagues about Sokki's request for the mini-nuke obtained through infiltration of a British research program. The Talons for Earth Freedom, which Sokki controlled with increasing directness, had shown outstanding efficiency and success, but the request for the mini-nuke was nonetheless an aggressive position. It implied that Sokki considered his group the premier force in the struggle against corporate hegemony.

"If it's no-go," said Alypia, "we have to take it graciously."

"We? You're with them, officially."

She gave him her sardonic smile. It emanated from strong, olive features beneath wavy brown hair.

"Come on, Sokki. They reserved this double for us."

"Ah, the secret's out. We're a couple in the eyes of the world."

"Not the world, just the guild. Because there *are* no secrets from them. That's their purpose, their strength."

"And the potential two-edged sword. Yeah, don't worry, Lyp. I'll be nice and courteous either way."

Anton returned. He was a little under average height, with dark hair combed straight back and aviator glasses. He sat in a chair matching the small couch on which the other two were seated. .

"Before we get to the weapon, we should discuss the expansion of your force, Sokki. It develops that we've identified *two* new elements, not only one, that the members consider appropriate."

A yellow light signaled caution in Sokki's mind. Anton's proposal meant three of five groups comprising the Talons would be contributions from the guild. His status as founder and leader might be compromised. On the other hand, his receiving the mini-nuke was apparently contingent on this expansion.

"You mentioned a group–an element–in the East before. Where's this second one out of?"

"It's not so much a group as an individual, a very rich one, out of Texas. The name is Rudocovitz."

Involuntarily, Sokki frowned in puzzlement. He'd heard of the eccentric billionaire from time to time, knew of the international success of the company he'd founded. But "Rudo" didn't seem to be trusted by the political power structure, so he wasn't a target of the Talons. He also seemed an unlikely ally, however, since he benefitted from policies the Talons opposed.

"Isn't he pretty right-wing?"

"When he chooses, yes. But that factor of choice–the capacity for caprice–is vital. Face it now: you have members in your original Midwest group who were seen as right-wing in their communities. Yes?"

Sokki nodded. The Talons were a coalition; there was no denying it. A coalition of individuals.

"So we trust this Rudo because he's a maverick?"

Anton hesitated, the term perhaps unfamiliar.

"No, more than that. A maverick might just return to the herd. No, our Rudo is a renegade. He is getting old and has long had all the money he needs. His remaining issues are not financial. They are with a great, intractable system that has rejected his ideas for progress, as he sees it. He therefore wishes to strike back, show that he is still potent, arouse the masses against his great enemy. Unable to do so with money alone, he seeks the help of the Talons for Earth Freedom."

"Who would benefit greatly in return," prompted Alypia.

"Yes," Anton acknowledged.

"I assume he understands," said Sokki, "that we're not being bought. Whatever he gives us, he doesn't run the Talons. Not more than his one-fifth, anyway."

"We've been clear on that with him," said Anton. "You are the head of the Talons and no one contradicts you. Of course, it's only reality that Rudo must have some input. He'll be generous in his support to the degree that a project interests him."

Within himself, Sokki savored the prospect of adding a billionaire to his forces. The added power would lose its meaning, however, if it changed the Talons' direction ideologically. He wanted Rudocovitz, but he mustn't appear too eager for him. He'd let the issue hang awhile.

"What about the eastern 'element'? Another individual?"

"No, a well-known group–notorious, I suppose. The People's Urban Progressive Union, in Philadelphia."

Sokki recalled news coverage of threatening harangues, a standoff with police from a tall apartment building. Noisy extremists, he thought, their violence self-indulgent, useless.

"Seems we're swinging the other way now. Aren't they Marxists, supposedly?"

"The 'supposedly' is well taken. They've actually refined their working philosophy, though the media hasn't caught up with it. Not as good a story, I assume. With our encouragement, PUPU will continue its transition to subtler, more effective methods of social reform. At the same time, they'll retain their militant nature as occasional operatives for the Talons for Earth Freedom."

"They're highly visible."

"As PUPU members, yes. But that has nothing to do with their role as Talons."

"Their own organization becomes a shell," said Alypia, "similar to the old Failure Club."

"Alypia did some of our contacts with them," Anton explained.

Sokki smiled at her.

"You're moving up."

"It's an important time," she said. "We all want to bring this together."

Sokki refocused on Anton.

"Okay, I see the balance. We're adding strength from the right and left wings, with them mitigating their agendas. It seems fine–great, even. But they have to understand that, as Talons, we all work together on a single series of projects. There's no side trips to settle anyone's local issues. It's all one big thrust."

"They've seen your work," said Anton. "Both new elements are very impressed. They will follow you."

His eyes were confident. Sokki absorbed the moment, feeling the power mount within him. It emanated through the room, out into the chill night and across Canada. His spirit had made its decision.

"Let's do it, then. Two more wings for the Phoenix."

Alypia smiled when he looked at her, but Anton remained preoccupied.

"Which brings us to the weapon," he said.

"The mini-nuke."

"Yes."

Anton came forward in his chair, his gaze directed at the coffee table. Just choosing his words, Sokki thought. The decision had been made earlier, though it might have depended on his acceptance of Texas and Philadelphia.

"It was a matter of some contention," Anton continued, "highly unusual for the guild. But then, we're not insane. None of us really want to use nuclear weapons. Only the maniacs we exclude have that enthusiasm. It was also suggested that, if the weapon is to be used, it might accomplish more on one or two other fronts. We take a worldwide view in allocating resources. In the end, however, your venue must take priority, since you are striking closest to the heart of what we fight against. With technical restrictions, the mini-nuke is yours."

Alypia placed her hand on Sokki's knee. He covered it with his own and gave her a wide smile of satisfaction, eyes half closed. The Talons were now the strongest revolutionary force in the world.

"What are the restrictions?" he asked.

"Well, the weapon of course must be housed in a secret and secure cache, proven adequate by past use."

"We have at least two such places, one in Ohio and one in the Rockies."

"In the mountains would look better to the guild."

"Done."

"Another matter concerns the plutonium core. It will not at

first be issued to you with the bulk of the device. It will be shipped from within the oligopoly when a plan for the weapon's use is in place, first being approved by the guild."

Sokki was tempted to give his disarming stare. No free hand, he thought. But then, they *did* have to be careful. No matter how much they trusted him as an individual, others in the Talons would have access.

"So I'll be storing a non-usable weapon?"

"Correct, but it serves purposes. It will save time when a plan for its use is approved. Also, if you wish to make modifications–perhaps install a timing or remote device instead of having impact detonation–it's right there for you to work on. It's certainly better for your technicians not to have the core in that case."

Sokki pictured his operatives tinkering with an armed mininuke.

"Yes," he said, "I can see that."

Anton smiled, his eyes turning up behind the aviator glasses.

"And then," he said, "you can also use it for a movie!"

"A movie?"

"A visual aid to demonstrate your power, like the one with the three soldiers."

"Blue Pond's effort," Alypia added.

"With this one, however, perhaps she can be more original. The other was rather trite. It fit the situation, I suppose, but the format has been used by maniacs. The public should see your force as a rational one, a catalyst for social progress."

"Which of course we are," said Sokki.

"Of course. That's why we assist you." His gaze drifted to Alypia. "So shall we order champagne?"

"Well, yes, I think so. You're in agreement, then, Sokki?"

Were it just the two of them, he'd make a show of procrastinating. It was part of their relationship. But Sokki didn't want to fool with this Anton, or with the formless, formidable guild.

"Yes," he said, "I am. And please thank your colleagues for me."

• • •

Evening had muted the fall colors outside the Galactic Retreat Center, but within the building light and colors abounded. For her first meeting as secretary of the Failure Club, Hilda had advised members to come costumed for a Halloween party, and about half complied. Bar and Ulitreé were therefore representative, he in everyday grunge and she in a covering of cabbage leaves. They sat about halfway back among the members, Ulitreé flanked on her other side by Megadamus, professional psychic, who'd come in a Merlin costume. Bar heard them murmuring at times, the flippant tones of Megadamus drawing glares from The Private, who patrolled a side aisle as sergeant-at-arms. In the front, Hilda ran the meeting while Mr. Singh was content to mostly listen. His own efforts to take charge had been draining, problems with communication confounding his good intentions.

"So," said Hilda, "since there are so few sign-ons for the Alaska cruise, I've suggested to Mr. Singh that we junk it in favor of a capitals-of-Europe tour. I think it will be more interesting, appeal to more of us members, and the percent of savings is the *same!*"

"Though the total cost is substantially more," Mr. Singh added quickly.

Hilda was wearing a witch costume in which she looked more like a pixie, while Mr. Singh was in his brown business suit.

"Yes," Hilda acknowledged. "But isn't it worth the cost–I mean, *can't* it be worth the cost–to expand your horizons, maybe change your life? That's what we're about, aren't we? Rising to new levels? Well, let's think it over, talk about it at break. But I think we should decide by the end of the meeting."

BEYOND THE FAILURE CLUB

The members hesitated to raise their hands, charmed or intimidated by this small authority figure who'd suddenly appeared. However, there was a serious issue on the agenda–whether to support assisted suicide legislation–and some members felt obligated to speak their minds. Unusually controversial for the club, the subject had been scheduled by Mr. Singh in a flustered moment. Rather than take a stand herself, Hilda yielded the floor to Mary Ellen, who'd worn her nurse's uniform as a costume and added the classic cap. The outfit might have helped as she made the humanist case, but she was eventually challenged with quotes from the Bible and hypothetical dilemmas. As the mood grew somber, the banter between Megadamus and Ulitreé was more noticeable, with the psychic sometimes adding an amused exclamation.

"Poof!" he gushed. "It went *poof!*"

The Private, dressed in combat fatigues, made his move from the aisle. As sergeant-at-arms, his patience was officially exhausted.

"You gotta can it, Merlin, or your ass goes outta here."

"Pardon me?"

"It means shut the fuck up. This here's serious. They're talking life or death."

"Oh? I thought we were having a club meeting. You know, as in social interaction et cetera?"

"Hey, don't get smart with me!"

He edged forward, but Bar came around and cut him off.

"Easy, now. Take it easy. It's not worth it."

Bar looked to the front and locked eyes with Hilda, who was watching motionless.

"We'll take our break now," she said suddenly. "Refreshments are at the back. Feel free to eat now or at the full party. The rest of the meeting will be light matters only."

"There," said Bar, "you hear that? C'mon, tiger, let's take a walk."

They eased away from the chairs as members started to chat and drift toward the refreshments. Mary Ellen made a move to join the two men, then stopped when she saw they were going outside. She'd have her time with The Private later.

"Thanks for stopping me," he said to Bar. "Almost lost it."

"Hey, no problem."

"Christ, it coulda blown up, maybe threatened the Talons' cover. Think I'm getting like Collins?"

"What? Hell, no! He was totally whacked out. You're just intense."

"Maybe I shouldn't come here no more."

He'd taken out a pack of cigarettes and offered one to Bar, who instinctively glanced back to see if Ulitreé were watching. They lit up under the starry sky, happy chatter emanating from the luminous building next to them.

"Actually," said Bar, "I hear they're phasing the club out as a cover. Andrew mentioned it on our visit up there."

"No shit! That explains those meetings Singh ran. Total chaos. I thought stuff was falling apart. Got me all tense like I am tonight."

"So stay home next time. It doesn't matter any more with the Talons."

"Ah, I got this sergeant-at-arms bullshit."

"Appoint me your backup. I have to come anyway 'cause of Ulitreé."

The Private showed a one-sided smile.

"Think you can handle the magic man?"

"Hey, one false move and he's out here in the cucumbers!"

They shared a laugh, looking toward the building where Merlin was holding court. As he turned back away from it, Bar noticed a pair of headlights coming up the drive.

"Looks like we have a late arrival."

It was an old pickup truck with the planet Saturn and "G.R.C." painted on its doors. It pulled into the one reserved parking space.

"The gurus," said The Private. "What the hell are *they* doin' here?"

The usual three monks got out and entered the building.

"Maybe we should head back in," Bar suggested.

"Yeah."

As they reentered the building, Bar saw the monks being warmly greeted by Hilda, Megadamus, and others. Bar felt relieved, having anticipated a conflict and call to duty as deputy sergeant-at-arms. Rather than fighting desecration of their facility, however, the monks were joining in the festivities.

"Attention!" Hilda shouted. "May I have your attention, please?"

The monks' leader, Sho, held up his arms to reinforce her appeal, quickly copied by Megadamus.

"I'd like to welcome Superior Sho and his disciples to our combination meeting and party," Hilda continued. "I invited them to thank them, along with our leadership–Mr. Singh, Dr. Xyntius who couldn't be here, and others–for the wonderful opportunity we have to meet in this sacred place and help each other rise to success! And after tonight, with your approval and the blessing of Superior Sho, we will no longer be the Failure Club but the *Success* Club, with programs for immediate improvement starting with someone from the Speakmasters Circle. It's a new time for us—time to look to the future with total positivity!"

Some of the people clapped and lively music began playing over the sound system. The refreshments table was replenished. Members started moving chairs, clearing the middle of the floor for dancing.

"Is the party starting now?" someone called out.

"Yes!" Hilda answered. "And by popular demand, the Alaska cruise has been changed to the capitals-of-Europe tour!"

"What about assisted suicide?" another member shouted. "Are we going to vote on it?"

"You can vote online!" replied Hilda, starting to move to the music. "It'll be on the website in three business days!"

She was turning away to Superior Sho, who again had his arms up but this time to dance. Members joined in, awkward but enjoying themselves, while others resumed their chatting on the periphery. The dozens of once-shattered personalities were melded into a colorful swirl of ephemeral joy.

"Total breakdown," observed The Private. "Know what I mean? Looks like we're outta here."

"It's all right, though," said Bar. "It was supposed to happen."

"You think so? Like *this*? Shit. I'm gettin' Mary Ellen, head back to the camper. You coming?"

"Can't right now. Ulitreé's dancing. I'll give you a call."

"Right."

The Private hesitated, staring at the dancers with set jaw.

"You know, I'm glad this happened."

"You're glad?"

"Right. Now we can get down to business. Full-time, without all this artifice. Blast those corporate buckos out of the water. Once and for good!"

He turned and walked off to fetch Mary Ellen. Bar watched him go, dressed for battle. It was true, Bar realized. The Talons for Earth Freedom would accelerate their progress. There was no going back; loyalties had been sworn, lives taken. Whatever the higher-ups were planning, it was sure to be on a larger and more devastating scale than what he'd seen so far. Tonight, in this festive setting with Ulitreé so happy, Bar almost didn't want to think about it. But he had to, he knew. His was one of the loyalties sworn, so the Talons took top priority in all his thoughts and actions.

He spotted Mr. Singh at the front of the hall, packing his papers in his briefcase. Bar decided to commiserate with him, cheer a man who'd unwittingly helped the Talons. Weaving his way through the dancers, Bar advanced toward the brown business suit.

CHAPTER 11

Riding from the Dallas airport to his downtown hotel, Andrew passed through the site of President Kennedy's murder. He noted the position of the infamous book depository, how a much better shot was available from the Dal-Tex building, as well as from the "grassy knoll." Another layer of reinforcement was added to his conspiracy belief. He wondered what Rudocovitz, the new Talons leader he'd meet here, believed on the subject. He'd already been a working adult at the time of the assassination, striving to establish the business that would make him billions. He'd no doubt accepted the Warren Report then, but over the years he'd strayed far from bourgeois ideology. He was now ready to attack the people and institutions he'd once sought to please, seeing them no longer as resources but as enemies of his vision and the future of his country.

Andrew arrived at the hotel, an upscale conversion of an early oil firm's headquarters. A placard in the lobby pictured a huge neon logo, a centaur, that had once graced the rooftop. Payment had been guaranteed by "Rudo," so Andrew was swiftly in his room, inspecting the drink offerings in the refrigerator. There was a separate sitting area and the chairs were thickly upholstered, speaking to expectations of opulence. This was the general theme of the hotel, at odds somewhat with the nature of the Talons and their meeting here. They weren't accustomed to wealth, except for Rudo, and even he no longer held it as a goal. As for the meeting, scheduled to include Sokki and Brother's Boy, it would begin the moral purging of a plundered industry.

The phone rang and Andrew picked it up. The self-assured voice of Sokki greeted him.

"I had them ring me when you checked in. We're meeting in the library at four."

"Rudo will be there?"

"Right. Bro was delayed but we'll start without him."

Andrew assumed that the rigid schedule was a concession to Rudocovitz, a kingpin of commerce with many demands on his time. The *reserved* sign before the library doors reinforced this view. On entering, however, Andrew found a man as relaxed as Sokki, albeit about a foot shorter. Though a billionaire, he wore a gray plaid sport coat that might have been bought off the rack. The only sign of his prosperity was his gentle aging. While he was technically joining the elderly, he appeared as ready as ever to be the salesman he'd been in the '60s. For him personally, at least, health care had not been an issue.

"Pickin' peas outta pig shit," he was saying to Sokki, and repeated the words reflectively.

Sokki nodded succinctly and introduced Andrew.

"Pardon my Bohemian," Rudo proffered.

"We were talking about going after rigs in the Gulf," said Sokki, "how it's pure futility."

"Thousands of 'em," said Rudo. "You take out ten, twenty, and the big boys just laugh at you. Collect insurance and raise gas prices to boot. So it's consumers you wind up hurting– them and the poor fellas on the rigs."

"All of which works against our purposes," Sokki agreed.

"So what will our target here be?" Andrew inquired.

"Mr. Rudocovitz–Rudo–has suggested a refinery. There are far fewer of them, they're land-based, and we can time our attack to minimize injuries. There's one in particular, one of the biggest–right, Rudo?"

"Half million barrels a day when she's active."

"It's currently down for hurricane repairs. Insurance has been collected, gas prices already raised. Another hit before it's running has to hit the fat cats, too. In their wallets."

"Leastwise it'll raise their premiums," said Rudo. "But the carrier mightn't even pay that second claim–cite improper security, disuse of facility–"

"Could we warn the workers?" Andrew asked. "Any that might be there, I mean."

"Sure," answered Sokki, "with the proper logistics. We'd naturally want to minimize loss of life. Besides striking at the right people, we want to make it clear who we're after, and who we're not. It's the way to gain support."

"There's plenty folks hate those bastards at the top," said Rudo. "Trick is to show they're not all-powerful, they're vulnerable. Then folks won't be intimidated as easy. That's where they get their power, you know: intimidation. Money alone don't hack it."

"They sure have their way with Congress," Sokki agreed, "even with campaign finance reform."

"Hell, it goes back far as you want to look. Tax breaks, subsidies, Gulf Wars, phony shortages, Vietnam–"

"Vietnam was about oil?" Andrew queried.

"Yeah, partly. They wanted to put rigs off the coast there. It's a bonanza under those waters. 'Course, Vietnam–that gets us back to JFK."

He eyed Sokki expectantly, but the tall man remained cool.

"He wanted to pull the troops out at an early stage. He'd signed the order the month before he was shot."

"He mighta survived on just that. Least as far as Big Oil was concerned. But the man was in the process of eliminating the oil depletion allowance, the foundation of our Texas empires. I say '*the* man' for a reason. It's because no single man, myself included, can put a dent in what's going on here."

Sokki nodded.

"I went through Dealy Plaza on my trip from the airport," said Andrew. "Guess it hasn't changed much since the assassination."

"Trees are bigger is all," said Rudo. "Funny thing is, away from that little area, the whole course of history was changed. Wars, concentration of power, wealth for the few–it all happened the way it couldn't if they didn't kill that man."

"Guess you're glad you weren't in oil."

"No, I came from humbler roots. I wasn't like the elder Bush, born on third base and figured he'd hit a triple. Electronics suited me fine. Room for pioneering, what America's really about. I'm proud of my effort, and grateful too, but now there's this other business, unfinished, and that's why I'm here with you boys."

"We're happy you're with us," said Sokki, "and I agree, of course, with your 'one man' observation. These oilmen themselves are part of a larger, worldwide network, but they no doubt have a lot of power in it."

"Damn right they do. The neocons found it out when they tried to privatize Iraq's oil. The oil companies resisted 'cause it'd upset the OPEC monopoly, which the big boys use to inflate their profits. They got their way, all right–knocked those neocons out to shitsville. Worldwide? Hell, they have the same lawyers as the Saudis!"

"Of course," Sokki encouraged, "this all goes on within U.S. dependence on foreign energy resources."

"Bull's-eye, my friend. I've been after the government for decades about domestic exploration, alternative resources, innovations to reduce consumption, abuses by these oilmen, et cetera, et cetera. All it ever got me from those lapdogs was a fat middle finger coated with sweet crude!" He paused a moment, shifting in his chair. "But I'm getting riled now. I know we can't afford that. We got work to do straightening these bastards out."

Sokki leaned forward, making a steeple of his hands. An artificial fire flickered in the library's fireplace.

"Yeah," Sokki said, "we do. And we need to do it in the right way–Talons style. Decisive, with everyone seeing the damage but not us. Yet they know we're responsible." He looked at Andrew. "That's why something like computer sabotage is out. Even if we could get to all their backups, they could say whatever they wanted to con the public."

"So we're talking explosives, then? On a refinery?"

"It'll be a big'un," Rudo chuckled.

Andrew recalled Sokki's visit the past summer, his plan to obtain a mini-nuke. Was this to be its fate? Sokki gazed as if reading his mind.

"The Private can get his stash here quickly. Added to that of the western group and Rudo's advanced devices, we'll send a message to Big Oil heard 'round the world!"

Rudo chuckled with satisfaction, Andrew understanding that he should keep quiet about the mini-nuke.

"We'll need aerial shots of the refinery," Sokki informed Rudo, "and some info on access, security, and such."

"Gotcha."

"Andrew, you'll have to make some calls after dinner. Inform your operatives–those we're using on the project–of my existence. Just the name and description, and that I'm overall supervisor on this. If they ask why, tell them it's the size of the project and number of people we're using."

Andrew absorbed the instructions. It appeared things were further along than he'd thought.

"Should they stand by to come here?"

"Yes. I'll contact them myself in the next few days. Tell The Private to have his explosives ready for transport. The full stock."

"What about the western people?"

"That's being attended to."

Which might explain Brother's Boy being delayed, Andrew thought. But he was confused by Sokki's manner, his apparent takeover of the Midwest Talons. There was something besides the mini-nuke that he didn't want to discuss in front of Rudo. When the billionaire begged off from dinner, it gave Andrew a chance to broach the subject. In the opulent comfort of the hotel restaurant, as they had cocktails prior to eating, Andrew asked Sokki what was going on. The other man sipped his drink and eyed him levelly.

"You're out," he said. "You're no longer in operations with the Talons for Earth Freedom."

Andrew didn't move, pinned by the potent stare.

"I don't get it."

"Sure you do. Dr. Xyntius needs help. He can't run our political wing all by himself. Especially now that he shares his secretary with the Failure Club."

Internally, Andrew did a reality check.

"You're doing the division already?"

"We're doing a lot of things just now. We're seizing the day, but with an eye toward a better future."

He raised his glass and Andrew joined the toast.

"You can stay and greet your old operatives if you want. But then return to your family, Andrew. It's where you belong. A secure member of society, beyond the risks, yet still lending your talents to the progress of our cause."

Andrew smiled at the words and the spreading warmth of liquor. Yes, it was real–the elusive dream come true. When they ordered dinner, Sokki chose filet mignon but Andrew opted for halibut. His taste for blood was gone.

• • •

Surrounded by raw pre-winter in the Rocky Mountains, the mini-nuke lay hidden beneath the floor of a converted smokehouse. The smokehouse was part of a compound nestled amid dense woods, the trees now denuded of leaves. The mini had been brought here from Denver, Sokki supervising its removal from a storage locker. Though lacking its plutonium core, the mini had already been used in a video directed by Blue Pond, with editing now in progress. The weapon was then retired to its nest beneath the smokehouse, where it would stay until shipped to the scene of a project, a planned assault on corporate hegemony. Brother's Boy had been asked to stand by, delay his trip to Dallas, pending word from Sokki on the mini-nuke. It had sounded ominous and, sure enough, as the Talons were finishing dinner and breaking out cards, a call came in from the Canadian: Brother's Boy was to leave for Dallas the next day, with the mini and selected operatives.

"What about the core?" asked Blue Pond. "The mini's useless without it. They don't need to make another video."

They were standing in front of the main house, amid tufts of dormant grass. The sea of stars seemed brighter in the icy air, reflecting infinite possibilities.

"I suppose they're getting it to him there, in Dallas," Brother's Boy replied. "I don't think he'd take it down in a bowling bag. Imagine if the airport screeners found it."

Blue Pond laughed, hunched in her jacket against the cold.

"I don't know. Might be some shock value there. It could have the same effect as an attack."

"Yeah, but then no more Sokki. He's the guy bringing all this together. This is more than an attack, Blue. It's an epiphany for the American people, the knowledge of someone besides the corporate brotherhood having some power."

"I like it, Bro. It's a new level for us. For the Talons, I mean."

"Right, it is."

"And maybe, when people see weakness in their oppressors, they'll ask more questions about shit from the past—wars, assassinations. The fear of questioning will be gone."

Brother's Boy smiled, turning to her full.

"And she waxed idealistic. *Op*timistic, at least. It's a new persona for you, Blue. Your own little epiphany."

"Damn, it's cold. Cold's getting to me, Bro. But it's not all that new to me, optimism. I was optimistic before. Long time ago."

He reached out and brought her against his side, the warmth of his huge body. She took a deep breath within his heavy, jacketed arm.

"Maybe we can get together when this is over," he said, "just relax for a while."

She hesitated a moment.

"Yeah, you can come to Alberta. I'll be a guest for a change in the resort."

Early next morning, the Talons extracted the mini-nuke from beneath the smokehouse floor. It was re-installed in the bogus photocopier in which it had traveled from Denver. The "copier" was then loaded in the back of a van with other office equipment, leaving room for Brother's Boy and three operatives. One of them was Maki, Blue Pond's most trusted Talon. Always ready to kill, his flaw as a person made him eminently suitable for this operation. While most of the Talons, Brother's Boy and Blue Pond included, had grave reservations about using a nuclear weapon, Maki could be trusted to follow *any* plan. If someone's finger had to push a button, shattering the well-founded taboo, he would be happy to comply. As if to balance Maki's presence, Brother's Boy also brought Ilena, the emergency medic from his own group. Their overall cause was humane, he must remember, no matter the imminent horror of this project.

The van pulled out while it was still morning, leaving Blue Pond in charge of the camp and release of the video.

• • •

The Midwest Talons had arrived in Dallas, Bar and Derek accompanying The Private and his explosives. They were housed in a budget motel a short drive from the one serving

Brother's Boy's group. Sokki had kept them apart to avoid attention, either to excessive people or to multiple loaded vans. The standard of invisibility had to be maintained. Sokki told The Private and company to stand by and keep a low profile, that attack was imminent. All that remained was the modification of a remote device being furnished by Rudo. He left photos and information on the refinery for the group to study, warning them to keep the materials hidden. Andrew had left for Wisconsin, so Sokki would call The Private directly when it was time to move.

"Andrew okay?" asked The Private.

"He's fine," Sokki replied, "working on other things for us."

"Shit's moving fast."

"It'll be moving a lot faster."

"We're with you, brother," said Derek.

Sokki gave a thin-lipped smile.

"I know."

He drove to the other motel and picked up Yves, one of Brother's Boy's operatives. A bearded, soft-spoken chemist, Yves would bring technical knowledge to the meeting with Rudo. Maki came also for security. While they were all Talons for Earth Freedom, there was a part of Sokki that could not entirely trust a billionaire. Bringing Maki, therefore, was part of covering every detail, another of the Talons' standards.

They left Dallas and drove to a small electronics warehouse in Fort Worth, property of Rudo. They were met by the owner and an engineer he employed, along with a large man whom Rudo called a "porter." The rich man gave a cagey smile as he sized up the trio that had arrived, as if seeing Sokki's reservation. Yet he had that reservation himself, Sokki thought, so we think alike on the matter. We're more similar than we knew, and apparently just as eager to get on with things.

"Where's the hardware?" Sokki asked.

"Hoagie'll get it," replied Rudo.

The designated porter disappeared behind some shelving. He reappeared a minute later pushing a cart with a plastic tub on it.

"Up to three dozen charges over a half-mile square," Rudo claimed, "simultaneous to the millisecond."

They peered into the tub, which contained a variety of electronic paraphernalia.

"Backup frequencies on the blow signal, remote programming if needed."

"We might need your man on-site," said Sokki.

Rudo turned to his engineer, an intense man with neat hair.

"Can you make it, Cecil?"

"With pleasure, sir."

"That was pro forma," Rudo informed Sokki. "All my boys would go to hell 'n back for me."

Sokki gave a brief smile.

"We'll also need to make some modifications."

A quizzical look from Rudo, then "Modifications? Why modifications? This is all according to specs."

"I'm sure it is, but the specs have changed. We're looking at a more focused detonation, rather than a wide area of discharges."

"But this is a refinery. You need to spread your charges for total destruction. Isn't that what we're after?"

"We'll get that and more. The first blast will trigger a second whose repercussions will be felt world-wide. I'm talking psychological value, of course. Pardon the hyperbole."

Rudo quickly understood, eyed Sokki candidly.

"You coulda let me in the loop," he said softly.

"There wasn't any loop. Let's step in the office there and I'll explain."

Rudo instructed his engineer to begin working with Yves on the modifications. The two leaders then withdrew to a windowed cubicle.

"Actually," said Sokki, "I wasn't sure myself it was going down till I received the core, right here in Dallas."

"From your backers, the internationals?"

"Right. Without the plutonium, we'd have gone with the conventional explosives."

"So it was tell on a need-to-know basis. I can appreciate that. But what about Andrew? He doesn't know?"

"He knows it's possible. He accepted it in theory as necessary for our cause, though it conflicts with his personal values. He's deeply idealistic, which I respect, but I didn't want his ideals on-site for this attack. With you, Rudo, it's the opposite. You're a true conservative, the classic kind, not the trashy current variety. You've opposed nuclear weapons, advocated stability, so I didn't want to present this to you in any general way. Now that you can see its value to our cause–this one specific attack, I mean–I feel I can count on your pragmatism to see us through to victory."

Rudo listened soberly, showing only a flicker of pleasure at the "true conservative" label.

"I assume," he said, "we're talking about a smaller-scale nuke, with concomitant reduction in after-effects?"

"Little to none outside the refinery area."

Rudo looked out toward the other Talons.

"Seems I'm winding up with a bit part in this, Sokki. You didn't need my kind of resources for a *prelim* explosion."

"Maybe not," the Canadian acknowledged. "But there's a long road ahead after this project. Your resources will be intrinsic to our success, on both the military and political fronts. That's where Andrew's heading now, to join Dr. Xyntius in our new political wing. With your financing, Rudo, they'll match the campaign funding of any opponent and legitimize the power of the Talons for Earth Freedom."

• • •

From the restaurant parking lot, the contingent of Talons had an unobstructed view of the refinery that marked the coastline. Bar and The Private sat in the van's front seat, Ilena in the back, with Cecil outside talking on his cell phone. A portion of The Private's explosives remained in the cargo, the rest currently being placed in the refinery. Yves and Brother's Boy would be at the other end of Cecil's call, assembling the components of destruction while Derek and Maki stood guard. They'd entered the huge complex in an electrical supplies truck emblazoned with the logo of one of Rudo's competitors.

"I never liked standby, being on backup," said The Private. "Better to be in there setting charges. I don't get this using just one unit, all this unused firepower here. Look at the size of that gig! You gotta give it all you got!" He turned around to Ilena. "Help me out on this?"

"I'm sure Brother's Boy knows what he's doing. We had that project with the mining company before we joined you guys. He's solid as they come, believe me."

The Private turned back to the view.

"Yeah, but it's Sokki got us hanging here. How we gonna get'm this extra stuff if they need it? I mean timely, not all confused."

"Don't worry about it," said Ilena. "You won't have to."

The Private turned again.

"Oh, yeah? You got the advantage on us, partner?"

"Just don't quote me."

"I guess we'll find out anyway," Bar interceded. "We've always done fine just following our plans, covering every detail."

"Every detail, yeah," said The Private. "Follow the specs." He shot a smile at Ilena. "Don't tell me *nothin'*!"

Bar's gaze drifted over the panorama of the refinery. There were numerous groups of large tanks in which crude oil and refined products were stored. A network of pipelines connected the tanks to a complex of refining plants and distillation towers. The whole facility was vast, and to Bar it's destruction was a daunting project. Yet here they were with explosives left over, not needed in the estimation of Sokki or the technicians. The refinery, awash now in the reddish glow of sunset, would supposedly still be destroyed.

"Could be some structures are more important to hit," he ventured. "The towers, maybe. Or the contents of certain tanks."

"Some'd be more flammable," The Private rejoined. "The more refined stuff. He could leave the crude and shit and still do a total."

"That's it, then–right? He just refocused to simplify the operation."

"I dunno," The Private smirked toward the back. "Ilena ain't talking."

Cecil was returning to the van.

"Installation complete," he sighed as he got in.

The Private grunted.

"We gotta hang tight till I hear from Sokki. We're still on backup till the truck gets clear. Shouldn't be no problem."

"Should I buy some more burgers for a cover?" Bar asked.

"Nah. I'll give'm five minutes then we'll move down the road."

Bar waited behind the wheel. A familiar tension filled the van as the Talons awaited their cue to move. Bar could hear Cecil's breathing, hoped he was all right, remembered that Cecil had a medic sitting next to him.

"Okay," The Private announced, "that's five plus a minute. Let's go."

His phone rang just as Bar started the motor. They sat with the engine running while The Private gave monosyllabic answers to his caller. He snapped the phone shut with satisfied finality, jamming it into his pocket and scrambling for his seatbelt.

"Back north and get right to the highway," he told Bar. "We gotta stash our payload right away."

Bar backed out of the space, swung out of the lot and onto the road. He was suddenly struck by the difference in this escape.

"We're not dumping our leftovers?"

"Guess not," The Private answered. "Guess they still need'm here for something."

They'd just gained the highway when it was shaken by the deep thud of the greater explosion. Looking back, they could soon discern a rising column with telltale mushroom cap. The worldwide taboo on using nuclear weapons had been broken. The attack was on the oil empire, the attackers invisible and unknown until they claimed responsibility.

• • •

The revelations began for Andrew while he was still in Dallas, on Sunday of the third week in November. As he separated from his Midwest operatives, he learned that his former role would be shared by Sokki and Brother's Boy. It was only temporary, though, since the Midwest Talons–their original group–were to be phased into a security detail for the political wing. This would leave the expansion groups as a military wing ringing the continent, with further recruitment to follow. Andrew returned to his home and his job sooner than expected, but with a sense of accomplishment and personal finality that he'd never known before. He felt closer to his family and more honest with his coworkers and the students at his school. The secret he kept from them was not so sinister now, and could soon be expressed as a legitimate avocation.

That Tuesday, as he poked around in the basement while Corinne prepared supper, she called him to come see something on the news. It was the refinery bombing, with fragmentary coverage of smoking ruins and numerous small fires. Initial reports indicated the possibility of a nuclear device, the newscaster said. Response by emergency crews was therefore delayed. Public officials were being briefed and any forthcoming statements would be carried live.

"My God," said Corinne. "Do you think it's a nuclear attack?"

Andrew had draped his arm over her shoulders. He pulled

her close now.

"They don't have many facts," he said. "It could be just an industrial accident."

"But they said it was nuclear. Some witnesses, anyway."

"People say all kinds of things. For different reasons. They should've waited on that and verified it."

Corinne shuddered. Andrew was reminded of politicians using fear of terror to control people.

"No related incidents were reported?"

"No," Corinne answered, "not yet." A hesitation, then "Guess that would mean we're not being attacked."

He sensed her hand on his back, moving slightly. Through the window, he noticed a swirl of brown leaves moving through the lamplight.

"Yes," he said. "I'd say you're right on that."

He brought Orchid down from her crib and they had dinner without the news. Andrew tried to sustain the peace and security he'd felt, but it was hard to reassure Corinne without divulging his knowledge of the Talons. It didn't help when, as they returned to the news later, assurance was given that there had, in fact, been a nuclear bomb. But it was also reported that–incredibly–there were apparently no fatalities. This was ascribed to a warning received before the blast, the refinery being shut down, and the work day having ended for the repair crews. About a dozen injuries were suffered in the vicinity of the refinery.

"At least no one was killed," Corinne commented. "But why would anyone do something like that?"

Andrew shook his head as if bemused. In another family, or on television, someone might joke about a protest against high gas prices. But Andrew and Corinne were always serious about the issues, keyed to truth. It was what had drawn them to each other and it continued to support their relationship. Andrew could only withhold what he knew, therefore, not make light of things or actively deceive.

"A nuclear weapon would be awful hard to get," he said.

"Whoever went to the trouble will probably want to take credit. Either that or the investigation will snare them. I'm sure it will be intense."

"Yeah," Corinne agreed, still attending to the TV screen. "Well, at least it wasn't another country. That's one good thing. It won't be another war."

Andrew held her on the couch, the room darkened except for the television and a night-light. Orchid was back upstairs, where they would soon be going themselves. Sheltered from the frigid night, they'd make their familiar love, happy about avoiding another war. How many, Andrew wondered, shared their feeling tonight? How many others would nurture hatred toward whomever had disrupted their nation's stability? The Talons had done well to issue the warning, but some skillful follow-up was needed to ensure that the right message was heard. He and Dr. Xyntius could not do much politically with a fearful, hostile public.

At school the next day, Andrew was beginning to lose himself in the day's work when word arrived of a new development. A video had been released by the Talons for Earth Freedom and was being broadcast on the news stations. Slipping away to the faculty lounge, Andrew tuned in the coverage. When the entire video was shown, it began with several figures in dark clothes standing behind a bi-conical metallic object about two feet high. There was a diagram propped next to the object showing a cross-section of its interior. The dark figures wore Halloween masks of U.S. presidents and the shortest among them, masked as Ronald Reagan, stepped forward to speak.

"People of North America," said Blue Pond through a voice changer, "the Talons for Earth Freedom have captured this nuclear weapon and will use it against the corrupt system it was built to serve. It will not be used to harm innocent citizens. It has a yield of two to three kilotons, very powerful but it can be concentrated on one large property. So we will not cause widespread death when we use it but we will cripple the corporate criminals who exploit you."

She turned to the chart and pointed out the plutonium core, the uranium cones surrounding it, the other materials. Though designed to explode on impact, Blue Pond claimed, they could also detonate it by other means. As Andrew watched, he drew what he assumed was the intended conclusion: the TEF knew what they were doing. They were equipped, competent, and eager to take on the giant business interests that controlled the world's economy. With the destruction of the oil refinery, people would have to take the video seriously, perhaps sense some vulnerability in the overriding power structure. What the viewers wouldn't know, Andrew thought, was the small number of the Talons and the shakiness of their support–the obscurity of the guild and the unpredictable egotism of Rudo.

The effect of the video was to widen the sense of alarm, with national guard units called up in various states to guard nuclear reactors and dams, as well as natural gas and oil facilities. There was heightened fear and yet, Andrew judged, it was tempered by the idea that these terrorists were different, that they carefully selected their targets and most people were safe from them. As this realization gained strength, it might eclipse the fear and open the way for the Talons to advance politically. How long that would take was another matter, and Andrew suspected that he and Dr. Xyntius were only the vanguard in what would be a long struggle for reform.

"Did you notice anything about her voice?" Corinne asked that night.

"A sort of hollowness? Some device, I suppose, to disguise it and foil the police. That machine they use to identify voices."

They were in bed, another dark night at the window with snowflakes like effervescence.

"No, I mean something else. Like she had a whole lot more to say. Angry, personal stuff. But she was holding back in order to follow a script."

Andrew recalled Blue Pond, the intensity of her deep-set

eyes, the occasional harshness of her gestures.

"Could be. I can't match your intuition, of course."

They watched the snowflakes, their random yet limited motions.

"Where do you think they stand? Left? Right? Something crazy?"

Andrew shifted his body thoughtfully.

"Hard to say. These labels, categories, can be misleading–distract from the substance of an issue, the merits of someone's position. I'd guess this group, the TEF, see themselves as progressive, maybe *are* to some extent. It's their methods that are at issue. Obviously. Whatever one's position, using guns and bombs to express it is going to get resistance."

"Yes, even when you're making the world safe for democracy."

Andrew smiled at her.

"Irony in the night. I don't think I'd place the TEF at *that* level."

"Is it really such an elevation? *Any* elevation?"

He hesitated.

"Maybe not. There's the net effects to consider. Focused, purposeful violence versus reckless devastation. The TEF's actions are tiny next to our country's wars, yet they might have some effect while the wars are futile."

"So where does that leave us, Andrew? You and me, our friends, all the educated and humane people? We're against violence, certainly killing, so what do we do with the TEF? Disown it even though it represents our views? Partly support it somehow? What?"

This was what he loved about their discussions: her frank summations of his own dilemmas. He could push them aside in favor of other people's pragmatism, but she would not. She kept him honest, making him fully evaluate the contradictions. He wouldn't often change his mind, but he could always proceed with more confidence, knowing that his judgment had been tested.

"Let's give it time," Andrew replied. "Getting swept up in the moment, in initial reactions, is a great way to be wrong. Facts will emerge, things become clearer. Eventually, we'll understand the TEF and how they relate to us, the same as we've processed everything else."

Corinne smiled and stroked him.

"So speaketh Andrew."

"Oh, do I pontificate?"

She grabbed behind his neck and pulled him toward her.

"All you want, Buster. All you want."

He laughed and circled her with his arms. It wouldn't always be this easy, he knew, to reconcile his work for the Talons with his personal life. He could distance himself from the violence, as could Dr. Xyntius, but it would be clear to all that their political agenda was that of the militants. That the revolution was temporary, to be followed by a settled period of reform, was a fine point that many would not accept. The challenge, Andrew saw, was to present their political wing as a separate entity and get it accepted as such. It would then be the Talons' primary identity, with violence simply part of its history, as it was with all powerful groups, with all nations. Shootings and bombings were often later seen as growing pains for societies and civilization. Rather than being abhorred, the bloodiest incidents were commemorated, sometimes reenacted.

With Thursday came more fortification of facilities, alerts to foreign branches, strong statements, and televised investigation of the refinery blast. Nothing beyond the TEF's video was discovered, however, so the saboteurs remained faceless and at large. Andrew applied himself to his counseling, responding minimally to mentions of terrorism. He picked up a movie on the way home, a quality mystery that he and Corinne could lose themselves in while Orchid slept. He was doing what he should, he believed, and harbored no illusions about controlling the Talons in the military wing.

On Friday as he went to lunch, Andrew encountered an

excited teacher coming from the faculty lounge.

"Have you heard?" she asked. "There's been another bombing in Dallas!"

"An oil facility?"

"No, a country club, resort or something. A big meeting of executives, officials. People were killed."

Andrew entered the lounge and joined some others watching news coverage. Unlike the footage of the refinery blast, these shots were from quite close, and the bombing had virtually flattened its target, leaving no recognizable structure. Any residual fire had already been extinguished. A smaller explosion, Andrew thought, but a much smaller target. Conventional materials. The Private.

"Dozens of industry leaders and public officials had just left the hall," informed the TV reporter, "or the death toll would have been much higher. The eleven presumed dead were members of the Council's governing board or prominent lobbyists for the oil and gas interests. The group had remained in the hall following the general session to discuss confidential matters. This was in keeping with the Council's protocol, which was kept in force for this emergency session."

So, Andrew thought, that's how it's to be: militant social action but tinged with vengeance. Twist the knife. And yet, the timing shows an effort to *spare* many lives, strike only at the core. That had to be strengthened: the focus on the practical goals of the Talons. They couldn't be politically credible amid a reign of terror. And he, Andrew saw, was not suited to be a terrorist. He was a husband and father and treasured his life in those roles. Sokki had been right; he belonged with his family. He had much to consider this weekend, a strategy to plan before he met with Dr. Xyntius.

CHAPTER 12

Bar sat in the darkened offices of Five-County Rehab and Counseling, idly surfing the Internet for reports on the Talons for Earth Freedom. Christmas decorations cast odd shadows and a light snow fell beyond the windows. It muffled the sound of approaching vehicles, so the first sound of visitors this night was a slamming of car doors. Bar heard them gain access past the security guard—quickly, so they must be policemen. He exited his search on the Internet and brought up the mundane screen of Five-County.

"Mr. Invictus? We're from Homeland Security. Agents Llewellyn and Figueroa."

The speaker was thick-set with shaggy brown hair and moustache. He showed his badge along with his partner, a smaller man with a pleasant smile.

"We were at your apartment," Llewellyn continued. "Your wife said we'd find you here."

"She's my fiancée. Is she okay?"

"She's fine. We just wanted to talk to you about the Success Club, formerly the Failure Club. We understand you're both members, though your, uh, fiancée hasn't been as involved as you."

Bar maintained his look of bemusement, but within himself he froze. He thought they'd been given a clean bill of health by the previous investigators. Had someone turned informer?

"Well," he said, "I've been to a couple more meetings than Ulitreé. That's about it."

Llewellyn leaned on the counter top next to Bar's desk, eyeing the case manager steadily. Agent Figueroa looked on placidly, not about to interrupt.

"According to the club's website," said Llewellyn, "you're currently an officer. Sergeant-at-arms. One of the two officers we haven't dismissed as either inactive or incompetent."

Bar's look of confusion was honest now. What was going on? In her enthusiasm, Hilda must have promoted him from stand-in for The Private to bona fide officer. But why did that earn him a grilling from these agents?

"I'm just filling in," Bar managed. "Till the next election."

He still didn't know why they were re-investigating the club. He was hesitant to ask, needing time to gather his thoughts, plan an escape if necessary. Llewellyn's dog-like stare was becoming irritating.

"What do you know about Hilda Diaz?" Figueroa spoke up.

"Hilda? She's the club secretary. Runs the meetings, the website and all. Acting president, I guess."

The conclusion came naturally, spontaneously. Hilda had a way of taking over, dominating the lesser personalities. Everyone saw it but no one blamed her for it, content to have someone in charge who lent significance to the meetings.

"You know her background?" asked Llewellyn.

"Background? Just that she works at the same place as Dr. Xyntius. Horizon State University, in Michigan."

"That's it?"

"Yeah, that's all I know."

The agents looked at each other.

"Well, we're sorry to disillusion you," Llewellyn resumed, "but Miss Diaz is a person of interest to our department, and other agencies as well."

"Her father is a rich and powerful man in South America," informed Figueroa. "Though they are somewhat estranged, she still has access to vast resources."

"I thought she was a secretary," said Bar. "The regular kind, I mean. Clerical."

"She is. She came here as a college student, but dropped out and entered secretarial school. To spite her father, perhaps. To show she could make her own way, didn't need his riches."

"Got married before she dropped out," injected Llewellyn. "He was radical, mentally unstable. They soon divorced but she had her citizenship, can't be deported."

"We continue to trace her in connection with her father, his organization, a possible foreign influence on our security."

"Her taking over your club raised an alert from our files. An investigation by my old partner in the sweep last summer. Low priority then, but not now. We'll need to keep a close eye on what Diaz does. After that business in Dallas, we can't have harmless clubs co-opted by security threats, becoming their fronts."

"Right," Bar nodded, "I certainly agree."

"Good."

Llewellyn looked around the dim office area, his partner continuing to watch Bar, smiling slightly.

"Tell you what," the larger man continued. "We'd like you to do something for us. For your country, really. As an American."

Bar waited without comment, absorbing the familiar, unpleasant ring of Llewellyn's words. The investigator leaned in closer over the counter.

"We'd like you to be our eyes at the club, watch Diaz. Let us know if she does anything suspicious. In light of what we've told you, I mean. Think you can handle that?"

"Sure," Bar answered, seeing no alternative.

"Good. And of course, don't tell anyone what you're doing or even that you talked to us. Okay?"

"Right. No problem."

Llewellyn pulled away from the counter and produced his business card. Agent Figueroa gave his also. Some explanation of the phone numbers, thanks and a smile for Bar's cooperation, and the agents were briskly off, reentering the ethereal frozen mist whence they'd come. Bar was left in the light of his computer screen, holding the two business cards, finding himself recruited again. The cards became irritating, like the agents' stares. With a spontaneous sneer, he dropped the cards into his wastebasket.

When it was time for his break, Bar left the office and drove to a nearby truck stop. Using the pay phone, he dialed a number in Belize, where The Private was vacationing with Mary Ellen. Bar gave a full account of his meeting with the investigators, ending with an encore sneer as he told the fate of the business cards. The Private laughed heartily, apparently in his cups.

"Hell, don't worry about it. Just give'm the old bullshit when they call. 'I don't know nothing, ain't seen nothing,' et cetera et cetera. Hey, that's rich, though, ain't it? Hilda being the mark? Takes the heat offa *us* pretty good!"

"Yeah, except now I'm stuck going to the meetings."

"So you were going anyway, right? With Ulitreé?"

"I was thinking we'd ease away, with the marriage and all coming."

"Oh, yeah. Big change for ya there, big change. Well, suck it up awhile and bullshit those lackeys. I ain't going back myself, man. It's Hilda's show as far as I'm concerned, *whatever* her connections."

"Guess we ought to inform our leaders, but how will it hit Dr. Xyntius?"

"I'll take care of it, go through Andrew or Brother's Boy. Too risky for you. Do like you're doing now any calls you make. We gotta stick by the rules, even though we're just security now."

Bar returned to work through the fine, windless snowfall. The counseling center was a dark blur until he was almost at the door. Waking up the security guard and proceeding to the inner chamber, Bar should have felt relieved after unburdening himself to The Private. But he was bothered by a change he felt in his workplace, his heretofore sanctuary from the bothersome demands of the daylight world. Tonight's visitors differed from the police who occasionally dropped by seeking information on clients. Those police were part of Bar's job here, and therefore part of his sanctuary. Agents Llewellyn and Figueroa, however, had come prying into Bar's own activities, a part of the world that belonged far away until he himself sought it. He didn't want it barging into his time here, yet it had and it lingered in the agents' expectations of him. His privacy had been breached, Bar thought. The compartments of his life were running together.

A few nights later, surfing as usual for news items on the Talons, Bar learned that Cecil–Rudo's engineer and a fellow saboteur in Texas–had committed suicide. The article came up because, during his breakdown, Cecil had expressed remorse over the deaths at the oilmen's summit. He died before he could be pressed for details, however, and Rudocovitz assured authorities that his engineer was innocent. A dedicated employee, he was the victim of stress that came from being an expert in cutting-edge technology, the stress of a highly competitive market.

• • •

Dr. Xyntius walked briskly through the campus, feeling trim in the new topcoat he'd bought with his political image in mind. Many of the students had left for the holidays, their finals over, but some remained and the professor was occasionally badgered for a grade. He parried each request with the same response: they hadn't been computed, they'd be posted securely on his website, please have patience. Further questioning was ignored. What could he tell them, after all? That Lauren had already left for New Mexico so he'd been making up love time with Hilda? True though it was, it was not for public consumption. Even with his political revival he was entitled to some privacy.

His wife had still been around when Andrew visited. Though brief, their meeting had gone well. Each of them understood the difficulties that lay ahead in their relationship to the military wing. While they could distance themselves from the violence, they could never repudiate the perpetrators. Their goals for society were the same, after all, and the attacks drew attention to the issues that would be their political strength. To reject the military wing, even under pressure, would diminish the validity of their issues in the public eye. They could study the methods used by their counterparts in Europe and the Middle East, but in the end their responses had to be styled for a North American audience. Through a scientific approach, Dr. Xyntius believed, they could handle it.

Like Andrew, he'd been shaken by the two Dallas attacks. Such devastation raised questions about the means being employed to achieve their ends. However, together with his protégé, the professor had decided to treat Dallas as the apex of Talons militarism, to be scaled only once. While they abhorred its brutality, it could serve as a point to increasingly work away from, phasing the Talons into a rational, mostly political force for social progress. With the New Relativity Party, they'd convince people and gain support without recourse to intimidation, the military Talons becoming shadows of their former selves. It wouldn't be fast, Dr. Xyntius knew, but it could and should be a steady process.

He reached the department offices, which were mostly empty, and found Hilda at work on the grades. She was sitting at a table near his desk.

"You have three, maybe four failures in your survey course," she informed him. "One is missing some lab work that could put him over."

"Ah, well. Let's assume he'd do it right and give him a *D*. I'm feeling beneficent today. Raise the others to *D* minus."

"One is super-low. It would be unfair to the other students."

He gave an ironic smile, then suddenly moved in and squeezed her shoulder.

"Little minx! Must you always keep me so honest?"

She smiled coyly but stayed with the grades.

"There are others in the office today, professor."

"There are? Horrors! I'm inculpated. All right, give the deadbeat an incomplete. When he asks about it, I'll give him some busy work to earn his *D*."

"Anything to avoid upset."

"Right, this is Horizon State. No further comment necessary." Having hung his topcoat, he settled in at his desk. "Of course, we also shouldn't waste our time, Miss Diaz. We both have *new* horizons beyond this one."

"Yes, *sir*–Senator!"

"Do I sound that ambitious? Actually, I think we'll start modestly this time, a run for the House at most. Andrew might run well for state rep. We're both from university towns, a solid core of support if we present well. We can link up later with other candidates, maybe bring them into the party."

"The *New* Relativity Party."

"Yes, new and stronger–much stronger. But we have to start modestly. That's where I went wrong the first time. A wild shot at the top and then no place to go, no resources. The idea is to make steady progress, not try to do everything at once. Rome wasn't built in a day."

"But the universe was. Right, Mr. Big Bang?"

He paused, showing only a small smile.

"Perhaps not. I don't want to be rigid. Science should accommodate alternate theories in areas of doubt."

"Is this the new politician talking? More skilled?"

"I should hope so. But I'm also sincere, Hilda. At least in your case. I recognize and respect the values in your background. I should have expressed it more before, I suppose."

"You're not just humoring me? The non-scientific romantic?"

"Not at all. And I don't see you as unrealistic. You're very efficient and practical in your way. Perhaps–I don't know, pragmatic?"

Hilda had turned in her chair, the grades forgotten. She eyed Dr. Xyntius steadily.

"Is this about that call the other night?"

"The new investigation, yes."

"I thought we were all set on that. My father has nothing to do with the club, so people can see and report what they want. Nothing will happen."

"Yes, the club will be the same."

"So what's the problem then, My President?"

Xyntius had to smile. He felt calm, in control, but knew he shouldn't toy with someone dear to him.

"Nothing. But sometimes non-problem isn't the best we can do with a situation, or someone in it. Your father, while not connected to the club–and it'll stay that way–is certainly a resource for another group, or campaign."

Hilda's eyebrows went up behind her glasses.

"Your politics? But I thought you already *had* support, lots of it. And besides, a connection to him would *hurt* your new party. Investigations again. You don't want that, do you?"

The professor grimaced.

"Of course not. You're right, I have ample support. What can happen, though, is that your supporters become insistent on your doing things their way. In that case, it's good to have other resources, just to show those supporters they don't own you, you still have options. I doubt we'd ever actually take anything from your father. We might never even need to control our supporters. It's just the idea of having him available. We'd be more secure politically. Who knows? Perhaps invincible."

Hilda gave a quick smile, then looked down thoughtfully.

"I don't know, Jon. We have our own issues, my father

and I. I'll think about it. But maybe we should finish these grades now. We've already put them off too long."

He acceded and they tended to the day's business. It took them past the normal lunchtime, so it was mid-afternoon by the time they drove to a restaurant. An early dinner, Xyntius thought, as one does with elderly relatives on a weekend. To compensate for the poor timing, he took Hilda to the fanciest place in the area. They sat with their menus among empty, cloth-covered tables, the winter sun oblique through distant windows. Hilda had been subdued, their usual banter in suspense. Xyntius sensed that he'd overreached himself. Beyond that, it pained him to trouble the thoughts of one about whom he cared deeply. He couldn't recall feeling this way before. Had he somehow grown today?

"You don't have to do it, of course, if you'd rather not," he said. "It was just an idea, a notion."

Hilda looked up from her menu, laid it down. She gazed into the distant, slanting sunlight.

"The thing is," she said, "I've made a life for myself on my own here, in this country. And it's totally legitimate, within the law, no matter what they suspect. I've been independent of my father for a long time. I'm attached now to this society, its institutions. I'm loyal. I don't want to do anything that changes this status, the status I give myself. I respect your politics and want to help, Jon, but as a part of my legitimate status, my participation in society. I don't want anything to upset that, or what we have together."

Xyntius felt a jolt from within. All inclination to involve Hilda's father had instantly evaporated.

"In a way," Hilda continued, "it's like when you proposed to me. We have a wonderful arrangement, but it's delicate. It depends on all the parts staying in place, not making a change that will shake them apart. And anything involving my father, Jon–well, it would be bad for me and bad for *us*, My President."

Dr. Xyntius felt totally helpless but maintained a placid

expression. Though reproved, he was loving it, basking in self-awareness–a necktied Buddha in a near-empty restaurant.

"Notion dispensed with," he said. "We needn't speak of it again, I hope."

"Yes," she smiled, "we needn't."

A waiter was approaching to take their orders. Dr. Xyntius poised to tell him they'd need a few more minutes.

• • •

Sokki stood at his living room window, taking his accustomed view of the Windsor and Detroit skylines. Behind him, the nude over the main couch was again shrouded in deference to Alypia's visit. The copperware glistened in the kitchen area, polished for pasta making, and the mirror was re-attached to the bureau in the bedroom. Whatever she'd bring from the guild, Sokki welcomed an interlude with Lyp. The Dallas actions and their aftermath–Cecil's death and the suspicion it cast on Rudo, the re-investigation of their old Midwest front–were crowding his consciousness. He needed to make further plans, use his formidable power with full confidence. Alypia–or rather, his immersion in her–would wipe the slate clean, remove the mental and emotional clutter so he could proceed with his quest. As she always had, she'd unfetter his soul.

When the buzzer sounded and Sokki answered, however, it was Anton who greeted him over the intercom.

"Is Alypia with you?"

"No. This is not a secure line, my friend."

Sokki buzzed him in. The guild man came up, then smiled when he saw the cloth over Modigliani's mistress. He stepped forward and casually removed the drapery.

"No need for prudery today," he said. "Rather absurd for men in our position, don't you think? Our role in the world? And we're not religious fanatics."

"No," Sokki agreed, "we're not." He slowly moved to his

armchair. "So where's Lyp?"

"She's in Philadelphia. Only briefly, then she'll be joining you."

Anton sat on the couch beneath the nude, squarely in the middle.

"She's briefing the Talons there," Anton continued. "Setting limits, really. Adjusting the scale of any impending or future actions."

"On behalf of the guild?"

"Of course."

Sokki's mind raced. He'd always known, or should have, that Lyp's basic loyalty was to the guild. She'd been working for them in bringing the Philly group into the Talons. Now, however, the guild was bypassing his role as head of the Talons. Resistance was out, he quickly realized. He owed most of the Talons' current power to the guild, and his original group had been converted to political spokesmen.

"Do you care for coffee?" he asked Anton.

"Thank you but no. I have other business in the area, so I won't be staying long." A hesitation. "I suppose you're wondering why we sent Alypia to Philadelphia, not contacting you beforehand."

"It crossed my mind, yes."

"Well, what about it do you want to know?"

Even were he capable of indignation, Sokki knew, this wouldn't be a time to express it. The work of decades, partially fulfilled, was at stake. He needed to tread lightly on the waters of revolutionary power.

"We're coming off a highly successful pair of actions in Dallas," he said. "In terms of *constructive* actions–militant social progress–it could be the biggest week of our era. I think that depends, though, on following through with everything we've got, the Philly group included, to let everyone know that corporate hegemony is finished. I went into the field in Dallas because of the size of the project, but I've fallen back now to my role of distant, invisible controller. I'm fully prepared to go forward, keeping to the standards that have ensured our success."

Anton sat back, crossing his legs. Did his eyes, Sokki wondered, show amusement behind the tinted glasses?

"Suppose I hadn't come today," Anton responded. "Would you be just as willing to recede into the wings? Or would you yourself be in Philadelphia soon, actively involved in a project against the financiers?"

"We both know one is due," Sokki ventured. "The one firm especially, its lead fund specializing in arms investments. Promoting warfare for the sake of profit, poisoning the politics of countless small investors."

"Oh, we can count them. And we can deal with them. We are sophisticated now, Sokki. You have contributed to that. But our actions, our methods must evolve beyond those used in Dallas, however much we gained there. We cannot simply shoot some fund managers, blow up some investors. More subtle, far-reaching techniques are necessary, which is why the guild decided to step in."

Sokki assumed an incredulous look.

"So there was dissatisfaction?"

Anton shrugged.

"Not really. The actions were effective, significant. Perhaps, as you say, historic. But it was noted that personal vendettas might be entering the picture. The double-digit deaths at the country club, for example. There was the scent of settling old scores."

"I've been in control of my feelings at all times, both when planning and executing. We wouldn't be this successful if I wasn't."

"We were thinking more about Rudo. But being right there working with him, perhaps humoring him for his resources, surely it was natural for you to join in his sentiments."

Sokki was silent, having no answer.

"The video maker, Blue Pond, also appeared vindictive in her presentation. She should have delegated the statement to an operative."

Sokki relaxed in his chair, resolving not to be defensive. He wasn't going to change their pragmatism, and he could certainly be pragmatic himself.

"So," he said, "where do we go from here?"

"Ah!" the other replied, holding up a finger.

Anton came forward on the couch and reached into his sport coat. Reflexively, Sokki imagined a gun coming out. But it was only an envelope, which Anton laid on the coffee table. Some crude sort of payoff, perhaps?

"Plane tickets," said Anton, "to Sweden. "For you and Alypia."

Sokki gave his slow, thin-lipped smile, refusing to be puzzled as he awaited explanation.

"It's a working vacation while we reorganize. We'd like you to sound out Dr. Lyme, your old field boss, on the techniques of financial sabotage. We do not want him back here, but we'd like some of his computer knowledge. This will also allow you to have some input when you join us on your return, in Montreal, as a member of the guild."

Sokki felt himself sitting rigid. They'd finally succeeded in surprising him. A lifetime of working as a loner had led him to assume he'd die as one.

"I take it Alypia knows of this?"

"Yes. She believes you should live in the *real* Canada."

They shared a moment of amusement.

"What about my business, the culmination of my career in society?"

"Your tax returns show net losses for three of the last four years, with the current year hardly promising. Nonetheless, the guild will purchase it for a generous amount."

"I hope that's coming out of Rudo's pocket."

Anton actually laughed.

"Then there's this apartment," Sokki continued, but he broke off as he glanced around it. He'd said "this," he realized, not "my," so in effect he was already gone.

"The guild will of course sublet," Anton proffered. "Take whatever you wish and we'll scour it for security after you're gone."

Scoured, Sokki thought. The environment he'd lovingly nurtured for himself and Lyp, though mostly for himself. Perhaps in Montreal, another older building–

"I must take my leave now," said Anton. "Alypia will come directly from Philadelphia. She will acquaint you with more details. I look forward to working with you in the guild, *and* to your relieving me of these southward trips."

They joined hands and Sokki saw him out. He lingered awhile by the closed door, envisioning Anton on the stairs, exiting the outside door. With the departure, with silence, Sokki could feel the full impact of Anton's visit, the guild's visit. Once again he'd been selected–drafted, in a way–with another disrupted life to put behind him. This time it wasn't as bad, of course. His fate was largely the result of choices he'd made. So he'd gone from bitter to bittersweet. What would the next change be? Pure sweetness? Nirvana? The ironic half-smile came, unconsciously, with no one there to be bothered by it.

Proceeding to the kitchen area, he fixed himself a scotch on the rocks. It was early for him to be drinking but he was on a different schedule now. He took a sip and then carried his drink to the bedroom, where he set it on the bureau. Rummaging in a closet, he pulled out a carton of little-used items, including a handgun. He eyed the gun soberly, wondering if it still fired right, but let it lie and instead removed a bulky brown envelope. He carried the parcel to the computer room along with his drink.

Seated in his computer chair next to the shredder, hearing its anticipatory hum, Sokki tore open the brown packet. He realized that more recent material would have to be shredded as well, at least what betrayed a personal slant to to his cause, but it was best to start at the source of all this. These were the artifacts of the latent Sokki, Arnold Peters, dating to a time when there was no campaign or need for for it. It was Peters whom the reinvented person, Sokki, sought to avenge, albeit within an agenda of other causes. The symbol of his crucial period, therefore, the document of his transformation, was the first item Sokki dropped into the shredder. The entries on the draft card had been made with a manual typewriter, its font blocky and archaic, the *I-A* smudged by an angry reaction long ago. It passed into the shredder with hardly a disruption in the disinterested hum.

"Join your long-lost brethren," Sokki spoke aloud, "the martyrs who went up in flames, the dupes who rot in landfills."

His college degree followed, the shredder reacting angrily to the thick document. It had been clipped to his letter of acceptance for grad school in Illinois. When he hadn't followed through, Sokki mused, they might have kept his file open, converting it eventually from paper to computer. Another letter was shredded next, one from four years earlier announcing his "honorary" college scholarship. There was also a prom photo showing Sokki with his date and another couple. He'd worn a white tux, of course, to offset his "grim reaper" mien. His hair seemed to have a slight coloring then, though it might just be the age of the photo. It was black and white. His date's hair could be dark blond, light brown, or reddish. Unable to recall which, Sokki consigned the problem to the shredder.

There were items from more tender years. He crouched in a team photo from frosh football, and there were track ribbons he'd won as a sophomore. It was all his height, of course; he had no real instinct for sports. They were cut short anyway when he went to work in the supermarket. His original social security card was here, along with the work permit signed by his mother and the school counselor. There was an award from before high school, "Sportsman of the Trip," from the summer he'd spent at camp. There was a leather badge that went with this certificate, but he'd left it on his bedroom wall when he left for Canada. Just as well, Sokki thought. The shredder might not handle it. He fed in the remaining items: a scorecard from a Kansas City Athletics game, a class photo from third grade, and the certified birth certificate of Arnold Sokki Peters.

Holding his drink, which was getting low, he stood before the pyramid of mug shots on one wall. These, too, would have to be shredded. Many of the photos had *X's* through them now, but among those that didn't was the one forming the apex. Rarely photographed, the man had made his fortune in the arms industry, triumphing financially in war after war. He was somewhat shrewder than the other merchants of death, however. He invested not only in arms but in campaigns of slander against those who might slow his profits. Peace was anathema to him, so he spared no expense to prevent or delay it. He spoke of defense of freedom, and it was freedom that he wanted–freedom for himself such as God allowed Satan.

You won't get away, Sokki vowed, draining his drink. I'll be working in the guild, but my every input will be fashioned to bring you down. That failing, I still have my friend in the carton back there.

At the window the winter sun was growing weak. The day's holiday shopping would be winding down, people heading home. A proper cocktail hour, Sokki thought. He'd pour another drink when he went for his tool kit, needed for pulling the hard drives from his computer. He hated to destroy it, all that work, but it was much too personal for his new role. He could ship the drives to Andrew, perhaps, but that wouldn't be fair. He'd be forcing an old agenda on Andrew as the lords of war had tried to force one on Peters. He and the Talons were social progressives, shouldn't repeat mistakes, and they should treat each other well.

He pulled the top photo from the pyramid on the wall, dropped it into the shredder, and continued on to the kitchen with his glass of reduced ice cubes.

EPILOGUE

Alain woke early in his off-campus apartment, blinking against the dawn light that raised a glow from Okkura's shoulder. Honey-gold, he thought. He'd shut the blinds and let her sleep while he prepared for his appointment. She'd been through a lot in recent times and he was grateful to her for coming here. He'd needed someone. She had, too, after her life in Sweden became too crowded for comfort. Dr. Lyme had been followed by his family, and then by a Canadian couple, so Okkura was the odd person out. Still, Alain thought, she could have gone anywhere but chose to come here, so he was grateful. A new dimension was added to his life as a pre-med student, and his involvement with the Failure/Success Club was vindicated. Even if this relationship were all it yielded, he'd been correct in joining. Their fields barely touched, massage and pre-med, yet the club had proven a catalyst—for discussion and now this.

He adjusted the blinds and moved out to the kitchen to make coffee. He'd make a full pot today, needing full alertness for his meeting with the dean of students. Starting the New Relativists as a campus organization was important to him. He was happy that Dr. Xyntius had reentered politics, especially when things were in such chaos under the major parties. He wanted to be part of the movement, however small, so the campus New Relativists were an obvious move.

Okkura came out as he prepared to leave. She wore a multicolored robe and blinked in the sunlight.

"Early start today?"

"My appointment with the dean, to get approval for the campus group."

"Oh, yeah. Mm, coffee. Did you eat?"

"Later. I have to be on time. Don't want to give them any excuse to turn me down."

"Cover every detail, huh?"

"Yes."

She smiled wanly beneath her tousled, reddish-blond hair. She approached and kissed him, briefly but as much with her breasts and thighs as with her lips.

"Good luck."

The sun blazed off new-fallen snow as he made the short drive to campus and administration building. His dark hair wafted in a chill breeze as he exited and approached the old building. He recalled the investigators from Homeland Security. A fine young man, they'd called him. Why should he be involved with something like the Failure Club? The dean likely felt the same way, about the club and now this political party. The answer, he'd come to realize, is that it isn't enough to be a fine young man. You had to stand ready to admit the weaknesses, the evil in your society, even at personal cost, and support the heroic people who strove to correct things.

"Your application materials appear to be complete," said the dean, Dr. de Vlieger. He was bald and complacent in expression. "Notwithstanding, I have a few questions. We can't simply rubber-stamp new organizations, particularly in times like these."

"I understand," said Alain.

"I have only one reservation, actually, but it's multifaceted. It concerns the political nature of the proposed group. As I think you can appreciate, it presents an issue."

"Dr. De Vlieger, we already have the Democrats, Republicans, and Greens. Why should political nature be an issue?"

The dean studied him.

"Well, as you're probably aware, the founder of this particular party, as well as its antecedent, was formerly employed here at Weisbrodt. It's fair to say, I think, that it's *his* party, his politics, that you're trying to reintroduce here."

Alain assumed a quizzical look.

"So? Isn't that the *more* reason to have an NRP chapter here? Other campuses will, so why not the very college that saw the forming of the founder's philosophy?"

"That might have to do—" The dean checked himself. "You know, Dr. Xyntius departed under a cloud here, in strained circumstances. His was a checkered career at Weisbrodt, in the view of many."

Alain sensed diversion, but he wouldn't be sidetracked.

"It's his *present* work that should be judged, the New Relativity Party. That and our right to discuss and promote it on a level with the other parties."

The dean gave a patronizing smile.

"Yes. Well, as I started to say before, it appears that the platform of the New Relativity Party—its 'founder's philosophy'—strongly parallels the agenda of the Talons for Earth Freedom. Not that Dr. Xyntius or the party is involved with them, but the similarity in goals is striking. Inevitably, the connection will be made in people's minds."

Alain weighed his response.

"The crucial difference is that they use violence, while we participate peacefully in the political process. Using *legitimate* means, we promote what we believe in. If it overlaps with another group—their agenda—that's beyond our control and shouldn't affect us. We're the peaceful alternative to them, after all. It's more reason to support us."

Dr. De Vlieger nodded. Alain sensed that he might actually be pleased.

"And, of course, you 'overlap' with the other political parties as well."

"Yes, that's true."

"Hm. Well, I guess we're down to potential alumni reaction. We *are* a private college, you know, dependent on heartfelt giving."

Alain drew a breath.

"The college exists for students who are here *now*, as it existed for the alumni when they were here. So it should be our call what happens here and now. But if alumni are an issue, I'll be happy to put them at ease myself, dispel their misconceptions."

The dean's eyebrows went up at Alain's closing words, his smile clearly one of pleasure.

"Really?"

He leaned forward at his desk, assuming a judicious mien over the application papers.

"Well, we *are* a liberal arts college. For the sake of learning, our students' sophistication in the world, we should welcome the widest possible spectrum of intelligent thought. Don't worry, I'll explain things to the alumni."

The Campus New Relativists were approved on a probationary basis. They'd have the minimum budget, the dean explained, with no special priority in the use of college facilities. It was the best he could do.

"You know," he said as they parted, "I was in Jon's corner when he was here. But I didn't have much seniority, much influence. I couldn't help him. Perhaps, when you see him, you can mention that I wish him well."

"Yes, sir. I will."

"Good luck with your organization."

Instead of returning to his car, Alain walked across a stretch of snowy campus to the college chapel. Alone, he sat on a bench in the old stone building, relishing the stillness as he gave thanks. This, too, was unscientific, like his aesthetic appreciation of Okkura. But it was narrow-mindedness that had led people and politics astray. There had to be room for balance within the truly progressive man. Yes, he believed in science, but why should that necessarily exclude the spiritual, the artistic? The pigheadedness of the present, with its insistence on wars and profits, must become a thing of the past. Science in government would do the job, but within that solution must be tolerance for other thought. The solution would then be a hybrid of all that was best in society. It would thus be far stronger than the current structure, which was held together by lies and constantly defended itself with appeals to nationalism and fear.

"Maybe you should run for something yourself," said Okkura that night.

"No," Alain answered, "I'm an organizer. A grass-roots person."

"Hm. So who's in-between those in the limelight and you at the roots?"

"Well, the issues. And our principles, what we stand for."

"But what people? Who's in there besides candidates and grunts?"

He smiled at her across the pillows.

"People like you. Inspirations. The ones we do it all for."

She propped herself on one elbow, facing him in semidark, then rushed at him with all her warmth.

• • •

The Arts Building was fully lit in the mild spring evening, the rally inside continuing, but Okkura and Mary Ellen walked together outside, across the campus lawns. They could still hear the speech of the NRP's candidate for governor, as well as shouted student responses, since the doors were propped open. The two women had left Alain sitting next to the podium, Dr.

De Vlieger providing faculty presence nearby. It was a promising event for Alain's group and the party, but the two female Talons needed to steal some time together.

"I'm sure he appreciates your coming," Okkura was saying, "a fellow medical person and all. He's very sincere but–sometimes–he sort of needs a boost in confidence."

"No problem. I'm just over in Columbus. Call anytime."

"Thanks. But you know, Mary Ellen, I guess it was really myself I dragged you here to see."

The other woman stopped and looked at her.

"I never really thanked you for helping me in Illinois."

"It was part of my role at the time, Okkura. My commitment to the Talons. Sorry it didn't work out later."

"Sweden, yes. But you couldn't have foreseen. Neither could I."

They moved to a stone bench and sat down, facing the Arts Building.

"I was wondering," Okkura began, then hesitated.

"Wondering what?"

"Well, as a nurse, dedicated to healing, do you see those things we did any differently now?"

"The projects? For the Talons?"

"Yes. Now that you're inactive with them, back to nursing full-time."

Mary Ellen looked toward the Arts Building, pensive.

"You're talking about the contradiction, how we wanted to work for a humane cause yet we got involved in violent actions."

"Yes."

"So many people must have faced that in the past. I think, in the end, each person has to resolve it for herself."

Okkura was silent.

"There was the broader purpose of the Talons," Mary Ellen continued. "They're surely right about corporate aggression, its political and military control. Oh, it dovetails with other schemes, but they'd be nothing by themselves. It's corporate power that drives the steamroller over the world. I saw it up close in Iraq, other places. The Talons are also rough, harsh and violent in their methods. But they're the antidote. Cures for diseases aren't always gentle. I guess that's how I reconciled my involvement."

"With the Talons and—your relationship? The Private?"

Mary Ellen hesitated.

"Yes," she said softly, "though that only works out so far."

"I admire your commitment."

"It develops with time. There's force of habit, not always a bad thing. A short cut around some issues, ones that can't be dealt with. Or that aren't worth the trouble."

"At least you both know."

"Know?"

"The Talons, each other's involvement. With Alain, I'm keeping a secret from him."

"Well, it's over for you, part of your past. Lots of people keep the past private, even with those closest to them."

"Yes, but—I don't know, he himself is so open. He deserves to know. Honestly, do you think I should tell him?"

Mary Ellen's jaw tightened, her gaze hard at the Arts Building.

"He'll work better not knowing."

Okkura was still. Mary Ellen softened and turned to her.

"He wouldn't *want* to know, for your relationship. He doesn't press for details on your arrests, does he? The prostitution charges?"

"No."

"See, he's into the present, what you have together. Why spoil it? Of course, we're also sworn to secrecy with the Talons. You're never completely out, you know."

"No, I guess not."

They looked toward the building, from which the sounds were subsiding. Okkura suggested they return.

"Is it worth it, then?" she asked as they walked. "All this with the party, the Talons right behind them?"

Mary Ellen frowned as if in thought, then gently laughed.

"It has to be," she replied. "It's all the world has just now. We've come rather far to start doubting, don't you think? Things would only lose their meaning if we didn't follow through."

They moved across the lawns toward the brilliant building, their celebratory dinner with Alain and the others. Spring scents rose around them and music could be heard from the conservatory across the campus. It was faint but enough to obscure the hum of myriad computers–the swift, secret messages among the agents for radical change.